MW01174481

# The Plight House

*by* Jason Hrivnak

PEDLAR PRESS | Toronto

ACKNOWLEDGEMENTS
The publisher wishes to thank the Canada Council for the Arts and the Ontario Arts Council for their generous support of our publishing program.


LIBRARY AND ARCHIVES CANADA
CATALOGUING IN PUBLICATION

Hrivnak, Jason, 1973-
    The plight house / Jason Hrivnak.

ISBN 978-1-897141-31-1

    I. Title.

PS8615.R58P65 2009     C813'.6     C2009-903391-7


DESIGN  Zab Design & Typography, Toronto

COVER ART  Tom Poirier

TYPEFACE  Dolly, by Underware Type Foundry

Printed in Canada

THE CANADA COUNCIL | LE CONSEIL DES ARTS
FOR THE ARTS | DU CANADA
SINCE 1957 | DEPUIS 1957

ONTARIO ARTS COUNCIL
CONSEIL DES ARTS DE L'ONTARIO

# The Plight House

# Introduction

**In the pre-dawn hours** of May 7, 2006, my childhood friend Fiona broke into the elementary school that she and I had attended more than twenty years earlier. She was dressed in layers of threadbare clothes and she carried with her, in a canvas duffel bag, the entirety of her worldly possessions. Fiercely independent and restless by nature, Fiona had spent most of the last decade drifting abroad. She had scrounged her way across three continents, always in search of the strongest drugs and the bleakest, most ill-starred company. No one knew that she had come back to Toronto. I imagine her simultaneously beautified and burdened by that lack of accountability, the terrible freedom of someone who sleeps where she falls and whose whereabouts are a perpetual mystery.

Once inside the school, she went wandering down the silent hallways, examining odd trophy cabinets and class photographs for a familiar name or face. In one of the upstairs classrooms, she stood by a window overlooking the schoolyard and for the better part of an hour wept quietly in the dark.

Sometime before first light, she went down to the front of the building and locked herself in the anteroom that connects the administration area with the principal's office. She sat down on the little padded bench where generations of the delinquent have awaited their turn to see the principal. There, after smoking one last cigarette, she took off her coat, rolled up her sleeves and opened her wrists with a razor blade.

I didn't learn of Fiona's death until almost five weeks later, the news coming to me in a letter from her father. He wrote to me at work and I remember the numbness that crept over me as I read his words, the sounds of the office becoming small and indistinct like something broadcast from another world. I must have read the central passage of the letter—the description of Fiona's death—a dozen times over without gaining the least sense that I had properly understood it. For all the lethal simplicity of what it was meant to convey, it seemed to have been written in code.

Fiona's father had not, of course, contacted me simply in order to relate the facts of his daughter's death. He wanted to ask a favour. Toward the end of the letter, he explained that the authorities had, in the course of examining Fiona's personal effects, found an old, tattered document folded up in the pocket of her jacket. The family had been unable to make sense of the document, but the handwriting struck them as being distinctly juvenile. They wondered if I might be able to shed some light on its meaning, Fiona and I having been so close as children. A colour photocopy was attached.

It was while examining the photocopy, a mess of loose and, indeed, childish-looking scrawl, that I felt the first faint shimmerings of a migraine. At the time, I told myself that the news of Fiona's death had been too much for me, overtaxing some vital subsystem in my always fragile constitution. It was a strangely nostalgic explanation, attributing to me a sensitivity that I had lost years, perhaps even decades, earlier.

I left work and sequestered myself in my apartment, just barely managing to close all the curtains before the full force of the migraine struck. I lay down in bed and let the pain wash over me. The headache raged unabating until sometime after midnight and, in the minutes before I fell asleep, I felt a wave of extraordinary calm. Old memories came unbuckled, giving a bright and bitter clarity to the written account of Fiona's death. I saw the anteroom in which she had killed herself and I understood the complete and utter hopelessness that her choice of milieu implied. No one could have seen her there, no one could have saved her. Whole squadrons of Fionas could annihilate themselves on the patched and weary naugahyde bench, no one but the coroner would ever know or care.

I called in sick for the rest of the week. In the days that followed, the migraine came and went, each wave of the bounceback more disorienting and dysphoric than the last. That's very much in keeping with my usual pattern. When a migraine stays with me for more than a day, it becomes progressively less painful but, at the same time, more phantasmagoric. By the third and fourth days of this particular attack,

I was lost in a forest of hallucinations. At one point I awoke and saw an eight-foot-tall man standing at the foot of my bed. He was peeling the flesh off his ribcage and crying fat, skyblue tears. I saw scenes of a city on the morning after carnival, the garbage and the trampled streamers so vivid and insistent before me that they looked the same whether I regarded them with eyes open or closed.

In a way, I've always enjoyed my migraines. They impose a different way of seeing. They wring from my tawdry, everyday surroundings the most unusual and overwhelming sensations. My favourite part by far, however, is the spell of lucidity that comes afterward. In the wake of an attack, I feel carefree and capable, with the bottomless lungs of a pearl-diver. The world around me bristles with the virgin ferocity of something not yet touched or tamed.

It was on the Sunday after receiving the death-letter, following four straight days of migraine, that I came up with the idea for *The Plight House*. Sitting up in bed for the first time in twelve or perhaps fourteen hours, I felt a sudden, unshakeable conviction that I could have saved Fiona. Thoughts of this kind must be terribly common in those who've lost a loved one to suicide, but this was no mere case of me second-guessing her family and her fellow travellers. This was different. My conviction was rooted in a secret store of memories to which Fiona and I alone had access. I'd never thought of those memories as something that could be invoked in order to help us and I probably never would have, except that the paper found on Fiona's body told me that she herself had been thinking about them in the hours leading up to her death.

The document recovered from Fiona's jacket was covered with the writing of not one child, but two: Fiona and myself. It was a page torn from one of the many notebooks in which we had laid out our plans for the Testing Range.

I met Fiona in the fall of 1982, on the first day of the school year. We were nine years old. Fiona was new to the neighbourhood and from the moment we met I knew that our friendship would be different. In the minutes leading up to the morning roll-call, she sat beside me despite that place having been assigned to another student. When the teacher pointed out that she had taken the wrong seat, Fiona told her that she and I had known one another years before, as toddlers, and requested that we be seated together. The teacher asked me if Fiona's story was true and, without hesitation, I replied that it was. I remember feeling an instant exhilaration at having been made a partner in such a pretty lie. It was a lie to which we never owned up, and over the years to follow we always spoke of that first day as our reunion, the moment we were brought back together after a long and painful exile.

By the end of the first few weeks, we were inseparable. In the schoolyard and beyond, we moved like creatures formerly cojoined, physically close whenever possible and, when separated, acutely aware of one another's absence. We developed a ritual of exchanging little notes and paper charms whenever we were parting for an unusual length of time. I came to believe that I could detect Fiona's warmth on objects that she hadn't touched in days.

The term itself—"testing range"—was almost certainly something that we borrowed from Fiona's father, a doctor who had spent the first decade of his career in the military. He was a tired-looking, self-involved man who took no great pains to hide his monumental disaffection with the trappings of civilian life. He fell rather easily to reminiscing about his military years, but Fiona and I never tired of listening to him. To our uncultured, godless ears, military terminology was like the English of the King James Bible. Listening to Fiona's father was a form of communion, a way of drawing into ourselves the vicious neutrality of *defilade* and *functional kills*, *rupture zones, fire for effect*.

Initially, it was nothing more than a figure of speech, one of those secret handshakes that children develop as a tribute to their own ingenuity. On days when our teacher had been especially boring or pedantic, Fiona and I would look at one another and say, "It's off to the Testing Range for her." When our spoiled and witless classmates read papers on how they would one day save the world, we would say, "A week on the Testing Range will clear all such nonsense from their heads." If anyone had pressed us to explain what we were talking about, we would have told them that the Testing Range was a nightmare-land, a place where hideous experiments were performed upon unwilling subjects. I think we would have agreed even back then that it was a place to which we alone could send our enemies and from which we alone had the power to call them back.

And we had no shortage of enemies. Our closeness was a perpetual irritant to those around us and made us something of a lightning rod at the school. The vice-principal who taught classes when our teacher was away would often refer to us openly as boyfriend and girlfriend, much to the delight of our peers. The older students were quick studies in the art of bullying, harming Fiona when they wanted to anger me and vice versa. The effect of this pressure, predictably enough, was to drive us yet closer together. We began to steal away from group assemblies and sporting events, even, sometimes, from class itself. While the other children drifted like sleepwalkers from home to school and back again, we began to carve out an alternate territory of hideouts and fallow ground, places where we could be alone. This was all new to me. Before meeting Fiona, I had been a fairly typical boy, lazy and insipid and shy. I was delighted with my newfound status as a pariah.

Our neighbourhood was a sterile, newly-built subdivision in the north-east corner of the city. It was bordered on two sides by industrial park, and the hydrofield that ran alongside the western row of warehouses was our favourite place to spend time. We spent countless hours wandering through the unkempt grass, the high-voltage wires singing starlike overhead. The field also served as the neighbourhood's de facto dumping ground, so it was common to find all manner of strange treasure discarded in the grass. Once, while rummaging through a cast-off steamer trunk, we found two porcelain-faced dolls, a boy and a girl. They were undoubtedly antiques, perhaps even valuable. We named them after ourselves and then smashed their faces with a cinderblock. We used baling wire to bind the two limp bodies together and then buried them in a shallow grave, our delegation to the land of the dead.

In November of that first year, we began to commit the Testing Range to paper. It started at Fiona's house on a rainy Saturday afternoon. Concerned that we were bored, Fiona's mother brought us some notepaper and writing utensils to help us pass the time. Instead of casually doodling, however, we spent several uninterrupted hours drawing detailed diagrams of key installations from the Testing Range. At the end of the day, just before we had to break for dinner, we looked over what we had done and became aware that our imaginary world had turned an important corner. There was no doubting the quality of our work. Our drawings were detailed and true to scale—frighteningly unchildlike—as if together we had been channelling the voice of some mad and heretical scientist.

From then on, we devoted several hours every week to writing and drawing the Testing Range. We made maps and floorplans and charts and manifestoes. We developed a complex shorthand, using symbols and abbreviations to stand in place of commonly-used terms. Whenever one of Fiona's parents looked in on us, they would invariably find us bent over our notebooks, working feverishly away at our plans. They must have thought us quite studious, quite exceptional.

The only time we halted our work was during Fiona's periodic bouts of illness. I don't believe that the illness itself was ever diagnosed to the family's satisfaction, but her father seemed to regard it as having a neurological origin. Fiona had been told not to talk about it, a fact which only helped convince me of its seriousness. In a rare instance of candour, she once told me that her attacks felt like having a fire trapped inside her head. She said that sometimes when she felt the prodrome of an attack, she would try to avert it by screaming or hitting herself or by destroying random objects around the house. She showed me a deep gouge that she had made in the dining room floor by dragging a heavy oak sideboard across the parquet. I did that, she said.

My custom was to leave Fiona alone on her sickdays, but once, driven by curiosity, I stopped by the house after school. Her mother answered the door and invited me inside. She told me that Fiona was in her room and that I should go up and see her, not warning me to be quiet or to keep my visit short. I remember being surprised by this. In retrospect, I can see that she disliked me and that her daughter's illness was intimately tied to her tolerance of my constant presence at the house. Despite all evidence to the contrary, Fiona's mother was trying to convince herself that the quiet, unspecial boy on her doorstep was a good influence on her daughter and an ally in her struggle to bring normality to the home. It's not without a measure of affection that I say I'm happy to have disappointed her.

Fiona's bedroom was on the top floor of the house, a slant-roofed little chamber with dormer windows on two sides. When I knocked and opened the door, I found her lying in bed, turned away on her side. I whispered her name and after a long silence she reached up and pulled away the covers, exposing her back and the open bedspace behind her.

I climbed into bed with her and drew the covers back over us. She asked me what had happened that day in school and I could tell from the sound of her voice that she'd been crying. I told her that one of the boys had fallen ill in class and vomited a spew of black lava onto his desk. I told her that the boy had collapsed to the floor and that when the teacher tried to resuscitate him, her hand had pierced through the brittle bones of his diaphragm and plunged like a hammer into his body. The sickness roiling within him then burned off the teacher's hand at the wrist and the entire class watched in fascination as she ran screaming down the halls. Later, at lunchtime, strange anthracite clouds had gathered above the schoolyard, raining fire and shrapnel upon the schoolchildren. The hellfires then spread throughout the city, incinerating every building in which we had ever set foot, exterminating every person we had ever known. I told Fiona that she and I were the only survivors, the world outside having grown too savage and bright and apocalyptic for anyone but the likes of us to survive.

After a while she fell into a light and fitful sleep, her hands crossed mummywise beneath her chin. I listened to the rhythm of her breath and slowed mine down to match. Anyone listening to us would have thought the room occupied by a single body, a single set of lungs. I pressed my lips to the nape of her neck and felt a thousand little trapdoors opening inside me.

Happy endings are dangerous and ugly because they drain the world of wonder. All children comprehend this. Those who accept the lifeless comforts of the clean and happy ending do so only because wonder so often comes intertwined with horror. What Fiona and I had begun to understand was that not only can horror be intoxicating, but that those who become drunk upon it lose all craving for the illusion that everything will turn out for the best. Though Fiona was fast becoming my entire world, my wish that day was not for her illness to disappear or for it to be vanquished by some sudden, miraculous cure. Instead, I wished that I too could have a head full of fire. I wished that she and I could wither and perish together, no sorrow to befall her that did not afflict me as well.

Over the next two and a half years, our plans for the Testing Range grew increasingly elaborate, filling dozens of notepads and sketchbooks. While the tests themselves were always violent, we quickly drifted away from the themes of pure vengeance that had motivated us at the start. We were far too interested in the inner lives of our test subjects to waste time on hackneyed torments like pulling out their fingernails or breaking them on a wheel. We understood that in order to induce the highest forms of rupture, we needed to develop a thorough working knowledge of each test subject's inmost desires and fears. It followed that, if we were serious in our task, we would have little use for general-purpose tests and installations, the best of each individual to be revealed by a more made-to-measure treatment.

There was, for instance, a girl in our class named Marnie whose most heartfelt dream was to become a concert violinist. We had heard Marnie play at morning assembly and while it was clear that her parents had invested heavily in lessons, our own opinion was that she possessed no special talent. Marnie also had, we discovered, a mortal fear of rats.

The test that we designed for her was called The Teeming Sea. It consisted of a simple hotel located on a backroad deep in the wilds of the Testing Range. We designed a special honeymoon suite, appointed in lavish red and black, and specified that the heart-shaped waterbed should be drained and replaced with a heart-shaped cage full of rats. Marnie's task was to spend a night in the cage. If she lasted the night without being bitten to death and without attempting to extricate herself, we would reward her with a one-year period of musical brilliance. If she wanted to have her brilliance renewed at the end of that year, she would have to present herself at the hotel again, this time to spend two nights in the cage.

That was the basic economy of the Testing Range: torment in exchange for a taste of whatever the heart desires. We wrote tests in which ugly boys won the love of the pretty girls by breaking their own feet with a hammer. We wrote tests in which elderly, senile neighbours were allowed one day of lucidity every year if they agreed to commit a prescribed act of violence against their loved ones. And because it was a property of the Testing Range to deliver ever-diminishing returns, each test grew more difficult and more virulent over time. The boy who had won his beloved by smashing his feet would likewise have to hammer his shins and his knees if he wished to keep her. The senile neighbour would be forced to commit ever more hideous acts until his loved ones abandoned him and he had no one left to visit on his ill-gotten lucid days.

In hindsight, it's easy to see that we were operating in very dangerous territory. By focusing the violence of our shared dreamlife upon the real individuals around us, we had made ourselves vulnerable to an infinite variety of misunderstandings. Had anyone ever discovered the nature of our work, we would doubtless have found ourselves in very serious trouble, not least because the benighted adults in our lives were incapable of recognizing the great warmth that drove us. The sad truth is that by investigating the desires and fears of our prospective test subjects, Fiona and I paid more attention to their inner lives than their own spouses and siblings and friends. With every test we designed, we shone a light onto the emptiness at the heart of our community, and, in so doing, drifted further away from the fold.

We continued to work on the Testing Range until the end of sixth grade, when Fiona received word that her father had accepted a new position in Chicago and that the family would be moving away by midsummer. We spent our last few weeks together in the customary way, writing and drawing and wandering the hydrofield. We never spoke about our imminent separation, a fact I considered to be a tacit admission that our work was winding to a close, that we would stand down, as it were, from our ever-intensifying antagonism with the world around us. Fiona's understanding, as I would discover, was the complete opposite.

On our last afternoon together, Fiona said that she had a surprise for me. She led me out into the hydrofield and down the path to one of our customary haunts, a little grassless area next to the rusted hull of an old electrical transformer. She reached into a hiding place beneath some pallets and pulled out two sheathed hunting knives, one of which she handed to me. I knew immediately what she was thinking. A week earlier I had written an especially bloody test called The Red Ones. It was nothing special, the kind of morbid little sketch that I used to produce back then whenever my mind was idling. I'd showed it to Fiona, though, and I remembered that she had filled the page with more than her usual number of comments and suggestions.

The test was a suicide pact for young lovers. It was unusual in that it didn't need to take place on the Testing Range, one location being as good as another so long as it was isolated and quiet. The test began with the two lovers sitting face to face on the ground, each armed with a knife and each intravenously hooked up to an unlimited supply of type-specific blood. On cue, they would then have to cut one another's carotid arteries. The idea of the test was for them to subsequently maintain eye contact for as long as possible. The external supply of blood would theoretically allow them to stay there bleeding indefinitely, but the moment either of them broke eye contact, the flow would cease and both test subjects would die. I specified that afterwards a red stone obelisk should be raised on the spot where the test had taken place, its height directly corresponding to the amount of time the lovers had maintained their gaze. I foresaw a world littered with these strange red monuments, each one a wonder to the lonely and unloved and a blemish to grieving parents.

For as long as I had known Fiona, my dreams had been rife with fantasies in which the two of us died together. Had she proposed a suicide pact even a few months earlier, when our immersion in the Testing Range would have blinded me to the consequences, I might well have agreed on the spot. But a subtle and, until then, invisible shift had taken place in the backrooms of my mind. Sitting across from her with the knife in my hand, I felt that the shadow of her imminent departure had already interposed itself between us. I felt that she was proposing the pact not as a form of union but, rather, as a means of avoiding the complex of unknowns that awaited her in her new home. Churlish as it was, I distrusted her. And I felt that it was beneath me to make a pact— any kind of pact—with someone whom I distrusted.

Ultimately, of course, Fiona didn't want to die that day any more than I did. What she wanted was a sacrament, something to mark the occasion of our parting and to close with proper solemnity the paracosm we had built together. We could have enacted a lesser version of the pact by scarring ourselves or by making an exchange of blood. We could have made the pact in spirit, holding the act itself in a kind of perpetual reserve. We could even have gone as far as unsheathing the knives and placing the steel upon one another's skin, the better to feel the wrongness of the idea and so divest it of its power. As the hesitant party, it was up to me to propose the middle road that would both preserve our lives and cement our friendship for the years to come. Lost, however, in my suspicion and in my sense of having been abandoned, I chose instead to throw everything away.

"These knives would be perfect for the test you showed me last week," said Fiona. "Don't you think?"

"I'm not sure which one you mean," I said.

"The one with the lovers. Cutting each other's throats."

"Actually, I thought that one was kind of stupid. Didn't you think it was stupid?"

"No. I liked it a whole lot."

I reached into my bag and took out my notebook. I leafed through to the page on which I had written The Red Ones and tore it out at the spine.

"Here," I said. "Keep it."

"You just ripped your notebook," she said.

"Well, it's no more use after today, right?"

"What am I supposed to do with this?"

"I don't know. Make a paper airplane. Put it on your wall in Chicago."

For a long time afterward, I thought that I'd handled the situation rather well, deflating the potential for ritual violence while at the same time giving Fiona a gift. I see now, of course, that what I'd uttered was a litany of petty cruelties. I'd implied that Fiona was stupid. I'd spoken to her as if I regarded her departure as a personal betrayal.

And, by vandalizing my notebook, I'd told her that I no longer cared about the Testing Range or the time we'd devoted to building it.

After that, we spent an awkward half hour making small talk and toeing silently at the dirt. We had planned to go out for a special dinner or cook hot dogs over a fire, but in the end we did neither. Fiona went home early, and, except for the fact that neither of us made reference to tomorrow, it was much like any other parting on any other day. I never saw her again.


We tried to keep in touch over the years to come, but Fiona cared for letter-writing far more than I did. I was deeply ashamed of the life I led after her departure and was reluctant to commit it to paper. School had become a nightmare. Grade seven was the year that my migraines started and in the lightning triage of junior high they marked me instantly as an undesirable. Lost and unsure of myself without my counterpart of so many years, I transformed overnight into the solitary, friendless boy that I'd always feared becoming. From the seventh grade through to the end of high school, I avoided close friendships and spent as much time as possible alone. I filled my mind with sex and garbage and watched the Testing Range fade like a dream.

Fiona, for her part, was terribly unhappy in Chicago. Her attacks returned with alarming frequency, their severity often great enough that she had to convalesce in hospital. Those hospital stays were something of a breaking point, frightening her and introducing a new sense of urgency to her already ungovernable nature. Whenever she was healthy, she made up for lost time by engaging in every form of rebellion available to a reckless teen. Her letters to me were always full of dark-eyed enthusiasm for the latest in illegal pharmaceuticals and fly-by-night underground clubs. She moved easily among people three or four years her senior, a skill that gave her access to crashpads and cars and paved the way to a precocious independence.

She left home at age sixteen and from that point forward I never knew where to reach her. Every two or three months, however, she sent me a hastily-scrawled letter or postcard recounting her latest misadventures. She told me about her failed attempts to make methamphetamine at a commune in northern California. She told me about the New Jersey divebar where she worked for tips and developed a bottle-a-day vodka habit. It seemed to be a point of honour that she would never attempt to conceal from me just how wildly out of control she had flown. For my eighteenth birthday she sent me a diamond earring, the accompanying letter explaining that she had torn it from another girl in the heat of a barfight. When I held the earring up to the light, I found a tiny rag of flesh caught scablike in the clasp.

The letters stopped coming shortly after I started university and, though it shames me to say it, I was relieved. We were on such grossly divergent paths. While Fiona was moving from place to place, a seasoned traveller, I was doing everything in my power to cut myself off from the world. At university, I skipped my classes and used the freedom of living alone to seek out new and ever deeper forms of solitude. I covered my windows with lightfast drapes and locked myself in my apartment for days, then weeks, at a time. I became obsessed with my dreams. I conducted experiments, varying my sleeping patterns in order to achieve maximum lucidity, then used my sharpening dream recall to fill an entire shelf of diaries. In a given day, I'd often spend as much as fourteen or fifteen hours recording the previous night's dreams—details as specific as weather and flora and styles of architecture—then go straight back to bed in order to start the process all over again. The cost of indulging my hunger for solitude was that I came to depend upon it. By the time I finished my degree, even simple tasks like going to the supermarket or sitting in a crowded examination hall would set off sudden, debilitating migraines. My vision of happiness was a windowless room in which I'd never again have to suffer the presence of another human being. It never once occurred to me that Fiona and I were equally unhealthy, equally ill-served by our respective strategies for living. As far as I was concerned, Fiona had successfully tailored a life to her inmost desires and I, for my part, was simply trying to do the same.

That manner of thinking sustained me through the joyless but tranquil decade in which, having graduated from university, I tried to make my start in life. Because privacy was always my first priority,

I had a number of false starts and developed a reputation, both personally and professionally, as someone who walks away from things easily. On bad days, my life seemed to be an endless succession of squalid apartments, indignant girlfriends and jobs that I left after a few short weeks. But gradually, over years, I gained a foothold. I learned to cut myself off from demanding people, even if they were precious to me and even if I thrived in their company. I learned that the only reliable way to avoid turmoil was to excise from my life anything that held the least potential to cause it. It was a difficult regimen, but I adhered to it like a zealot. By my early thirties, I had successfully transformed my life into a hushed and tidy room that was utterly devoid of event.

The news of Fiona's death tore apart my carefully-constructed little world. In the aftermath, I found myself wishing, quite uncharacteristically, that I'd developed the kind of interpersonal network that a person is meant to lean upon at such times. The distraction alone would have been a godsend. As it was, I had plenty of time in which to confront the trap I'd built for myself. Initially, it seemed like a gross inconsistency that the death of someone who'd been lost to me for so long should shake me so profoundly. I hadn't understood that even the most neglected bonds can persist across the years like something dormant in the blood. As such, I had no way of foreseeing the flurry of productivity to which those bonds, reawakened, would drive me.

I wrote *The Plight House* during the summer of 2006, mostly in the early mornings before work. It was an awful process. From the moment I started the project, I was driven by a grim, unwavering urgency that woke me up at four AM, no matter how little I'd slept, and set me to work at my desk. It would be fair to say that I wrote the book in a kind of intermittent fever: for two hours every morning I immersed myself in the intricacies of Fiona's suicide, then went numb for the rest of the day. Except for the writing process itself, which I recall vividly, I have almost no memories of that summer.

In the end, of course, I have no way of knowing whether or not the finished product could indeed have fulfilled its stated purpose of preventing Fiona's death. My feelings about its odds of success tend to change with my mood. I'm certain, however, of its rightness, its conformance to a kind of empty socket in the final hours of her life. *The Plight House* is the missing element from the night Fiona broke into the school, its failure to appear there no different from the absence of a stolen property or a garment devoured by moths. I picture the manuscript sitting ready on a clean, well-lit desk, a batch of sharpened pencils at the side. I picture Fiona noticing it in the course of her wanderings and stepping cautiously into the light, aware of a twist in the game.

She would have understood within the first few pages that the test was not written by a doctor or a parent or even, fundamentally, by a friend. And its coldness would have come as a great relief to her. I knew from the outset that the test's chance of success would inhere in its refusal, first, to sing her back toward a world that she despised, and, second, to use guilt as a straitjacket. My only hope was to create a resonance, duplicating both in myself and in the text the particular frequency of despair that was driving her toward suicide. I'm not sure what, if anything, it would have meant to her to experience that resonance. But so long as she understood that she had been seen, and therefore accompanied, in that worst of all possible moments, I could have lived with her decision.

As for myself, each year since the suicide has been worse than the one before. At this point, the life I lead is, by any definition, both very small and worth very little. *The Plight House* has been central to that process of disintegration, as time and time again I've found myself sickened by the irony of having gained from Fiona's death both the impetus and the means to save her. In truth, however, that sickened feeling is also my greatest comfort, supporting as it does the notion that I didn't write *The Plight House* for myself. Throughout the process of composition, I worried constantly that some hidden, selfish motive would contaminate the work, that I would finish it only to find that its true purpose was somehow to improve my own lot. But my lot has decidedly not improved. My rags and my tremors and this tiny, fetid room all stand as proof that finally, in this one lonely endeavour, my devotion has been unstinting.

I believe that Fiona was utterly unique and that the fierce little specifics of her personality will never be duplicated or recur in someone else. I suspect as well that *The Plight House* will have little or no therapeutic power for anyone other than its one intended recipient. The possibility that I'm wrong on either count, however, has cost me a lot of sleep and, in the end, I gauge that a little peace of mind is worth the blow to my privacy. Hence my decision to publish *The Plight House*.

You might already, in the course of reading this introduction, have thought of someone in your circle who you believe to be a Fiona. This individual could be a friend or a relative or, worst of all, a lover. The first thing you must understand, if you're to have any chance of saving her, is that she is much more delicate than she appears to be. Luminaries repel our solicitude in the same measure that they attract our admiration. It's for this reason that so many of them die at centre stage, depleted in their brightest hour, alone in plain view. Your Fiona will be no exception unless you commit yourself entirely to her care. Watch her closely for signs of creeping anhedonia and for coded, elliptical goodbyes. If it becomes necessary to administer *The Plight House*, do so without apology and without expectation of thanks. Her tears of protest may rend your heart, but remember the alternative. She stands to lose everything, and so, therein, do you.

The Plight House

# Section I

1. Childhood. Walking in the countryside, you encounter a dark rider upon the road. He challenges you
   to a battle of wits. Your intellect is keen, sharpened
   by sums and precocious reading, but the rider is
   confident of victory. He says that there is a subject
   on which young girls believe themselves to be great
   thinkers but on which none, in truth, are qualified
   to speak. It is on this subject that he aims to riddle
   you. To what does the rider refer?

   A. Music.
   B. Beauty.
   C. Love.
   D. Death.

2. Strolling the midway at the annual summer fair,
   you are cajoled by one of the carnies into playing
   a game of *follow the lady*. The carny places a pea
   under one of three upended cups, then shuffles the
   cups over the surface of his table. When invited
   to find the pea, you pick the leftmost cup only to
   discover that the pea has transformed into a small
   and brightly-coloured bird. The carny is taken aback.

According to the rules of the game, what prize do you now win?

    A. The secrets of the midway.
    B. Free access to the rides.
    C. Your likeness added to the waxworks.
    D. The right to join the troupe.

3. You are a child of simple forestfolk. Unschooled, the youngest by far of four sisters, you are left largely to your own devices. Over time, you invent for yourself an imaginary friend. His eyes are brilliant amethyst and he is your constant companion, a prankster and a maker of mischief. One day, he proposes to materialize before you in the flesh. In what form would you have him appear?

    A. A hawk.
    B. A boy.
    C. A horse.
    D. A dragon.

4. Two children meet in the heart of the forest. They reach into a hollow beneath the roots of a twisted oak and remove from it a wooden box. Inside the box is a creature that they have painstakingly fashioned from doll-parts and leather and the bones of dead animals. What is required in order to animate this heretofore lifeless thing?

    A. The death of one child at the hands of the other.
    B. The death of both.
    C. The death of a third, unsuspecting child.
    D. The death of every adult within a radius of five kilometres.

5. You walk down the street singing a song that you have made up for your own amusement. The song recounts the adventures of a young girl who slaughters her beloved in order to keep him forever by her side. A policeman overhears you and places you under arrest. He demands to know who taught you the song. What is your reply?

   A. "The god of war."
   B. "I heard it on the radio."
   C. "I don't remember."
   D. "The butcher's daughter."

6. At the age of twelve, you become enamoured of the boy from down the lane. He is an aspiring mountaineer. When you learn of his passion for climbing, you begin to have a recurring dream that you yourself are a mountain climber. Night after night, you scale an interminable rockface, your dream-hands growing callused and strong with the effort. Over time, these dreams must inevitably transform into which of the following?

   A. Dreams of falling (accidental).
   B. Dreams of falling (suicidal).
   C. A waking fetish for heights.
   D. A waking aversion to heights.

7. There is a star in the firmament. It shines on you specifically, like a fixed and dogged spotlight. When you try to speak gently, it makes you cruel. When you seek compromise, it drives you to new and frightening extremes. Were it up to that star, your life would be a perpetual state of _____.

A. Agitation.
B. Disaster.
C. Illness.
D. Upheaval.

8. As you enter your teenage years, your imaginary friend with the amethyst eyes remains your only worldly companion. Concerned by your lack of interest in kinship of the flesh-and-blood variety, your parents take you on a trip to the lake. A small sailboat sits tied to the dock. Your parents raise the sail and set the empty boat adrift on the waters. They tell you that your imaginary friend is in the boat and that he is going away forever. They tell you to wave goodbye. What action do you take?

   A. Jump into the water and swim after your friend, with the aim of bringing him back.
   B. Jump into the water and swim after your friend, with the aim of joining him in exile.
   C. Hide your face in your hands and weep.
   D. Wave goodbye, as instructed.

9. You go to the theatre. The play to be performed is called "The Portal." It is poorly attended, with only a half dozen spectators in the auditorium, and has received no reviews. As the houselights fade to black, an unseen figure snickers in the wings and you experience a sudden and overwhelming premonition of dread. The curtains begin to part. Which of the following now pours off the stage and into the auditorium?

A. Seawater.
B. Cockroaches.
C. Rats.
D. A blinding white light.

10. On your seventeenth birthday, you receive a package in the mail. Inside the package are a letter and a diamond ring. The letter reads, "Hello. I am a virus and you have just unleashed me. To vaccinate yourself, place ring on finger." With what aim has the letter's author sent you this package?

A. To frighten you.
B. To propose marriage.
C. To protect you.
D. To start an epidemic.

11. A storm is gathering. It darkens the sky above your home and batters the walls with fierce, cold winds. At night, as you try to sleep, you hear the voices of children overhead, their songs and rhymes carried upon the wind like sounds from a flying schoolyard. In the morning, there is thunder and lightning and the downpour proper begins. The land is pelted with rain and which of the following?

A. Broken dolls.
B. Storybooks.
C. Leaflets on which are printed the faces of missing children.
D. Baby teeth.

12. Late one night, under the brightest of lights, you disrobe in front of the mirror. You are the very image of female radiance. Your skin is flawless, your figure

a trumpet blast of sexual promise. On your back, just above the shoulder blades, two mounds of feathered bone have begun to protrude upward through the skin. These are your wings. Left to grow unfettered, what physiological effect will they have?

- A. They will cause your hair to fall out.
- B. They will deprive your skin of its lustre and elasticity.
- C. They will rob you of the ability to swim.
- D. They will make you barren.

13. You have a migraine. The aura cuts glasslike into your field of vision and the pain, once entrenched, lasts for more than a week. Upon recovery, you find your bedroom filled with strange pilgrims. Your caregivers explain that these pilgrims have come to your bedside from distant lands after hearing word of your special powers. What wonder have you allegedly performed whilst incapacitated?

- A. You have spoken in tongues.
- B. You have levitated.
- C. You have belched forth a rare and poisonous snake.
- D. You have built a cathedral.

14. In the days leading up to the autumnal equinox, the boy from down the lane commits suicide. His sister finds him in the bathtub, his thighs slashed open with a serrated knife. Though you had only ever admired him from afar, never speaking with him save to exchange a polite word of greeting, the boy has addressed his suicide letter to you. It reads,

simply, "You are mine." Which of the following most accurately describes the intended purpose of this message?

    A. It is a curse, wholly malevolent in nature.
    B. It is a warning that you too will soon die by your own hand.
    C. It is a call for you to fulfill your end of an imagined, erotomanic pact.
    D. It is an attempt to refigure the act of self-murder as a vow of endless chastity.

15. In the weeks following the boy's death, you are troubled at all hours by dark and harrowing visions. In sudden, dreamlike fits of hallucination, you see yourself bleeding from self-inflicted wounds or drowning at the bottom of a river. Alarmed by your rapid mental deterioration, your doctor volunteers you for a harsh and highly experimental treatment at a vanguard facility known as The Plight House. Why do you not fear the near-legendary harshness of the treatment conducted therein?

    A. Simple desperation.
    B. Simple indifference.
    C. You crave that specific category of self-knowledge that hardship alone can bestow.
    D. You believe that ordeal alone can reactivate your will to survive.

16. The door to The Plight House lies hidden in a quarry on the grounds of an abandoned military base. Arriving at the site under the last light of day, you find that the quarry has been flooded. The floodwater is stagnant and visibly polluted, with clumps of

amorphous matter floating sewagelike beneath the
surface. As you hold your breath and dive into the
water, by which of the following is your mind's eye
assailed?

- A. Visions of a drowned city.
- B. Memories of childhood.
- C. A tapestry of detailed but random
  hallucinations.
- D. The unmoored dreams and nightmares of
  those who have gone before you.

17. In the first chamber of The Plight House, preserved
under glass, is the document known as the South
Sea Hag Letter. The document was discovered in the
waters of the Pacific Gyre, sealed in a bottle and tied
to the almost completely decomposed corpse of an
unidentified woman. Your task is to memorize the
document in its entirety. The contents of the South
Sea Hag Letter are fabled to induce in the reader a
proclivity for which of the following?

- A. Drug addiction.
- B. Sexual obsession.
- C. Paranoia.
- D. Self-mutilation.

18. In the second chamber of The Plight House, a
capacious video screen displays a live image
transmitted from a distant wing of the installation.
In the image, a man with no face lies unconscious
upon a strip of artificial turf. The man is thin and
wild of demeanour, twitching in his sleep like the
recipient of a feverdream. Your task is to awaken

him. What tribute must you deposit at the foot of the video screen in order to accomplish this task?

    A. A litre of blood.

    B. A dead falcon.

    C. Your heart.

    D. 750 milligrams of hair.

19. I awaken in a grassy field, dressed in rags. On my left inner forearm is tattooed a cluster of seventeen stars. Two of the tattooed stars are still fresh. As I wander and attempt to gain my bearings in this unfamiliar place, I find two armed militiamen lying dead at the foot of a blasted oak. Their bodies have been crushed by hands of monstrous strength. Who am I?

    A. A hapless drifter.

    B. A vengeful widower.

    C. The lord high executioner of this district.

    D. An indiscriminate devourer of human souls.

20. Walking away from the tree and corpses, I find a roadside vendor selling small bottles of homemade liquor. The liquor is pearly grey in colour, with a strange metallic sheen. The vendor informs me that it is made from apples grown in subterranean orchards. I buy a bottle with my pocketchange and drink it on the spot. Drunkenness agrees with me. My deep interest in human intoxication will ultimately lead to my death in which of the following locales?

    A. The bathroom of a rooming house.

    B. The basement of a pharmaceutical company.

    C. A bullet-riddled shack.

    D. A subterranean orchard.

21. In later years, I become an engineer of mind-altering drugs. I build a house in the countryside, far from the prying eyes of neighbours and crowds. In my house, I am free to work at all hours of the night and to pursue my vocation without fear of reprisal. Under these conditions I soon succeed in crafting drugs of untold addictive potency. Which of the following would be the most suitable inscription for the lintel of my home?

    A. "Down with sleep."
    B. "Let nothing more come between us."
    C. "Ring bell for service."
    D. "This is not a door."

22. An excerpt from the South Sea Hag Letter:

    The constellation known as the Scavenger is visible in this hemisphere between the months of December and May. When comets cross the Scavenger's torso, horses die in their sleep and children are born with deformities of the spine. He is flanked by the Anorexic to his left and to his right the Necrofile. The stars that compose his face glow brighter when I disrobe.

    According to the author's reconfiguration of the night sky, what constellations are situated on either side of the Anorexic and the Necrofile, respectively?

    A. The Arsonist and the Two-Headed Baby.
    B. The Pole Dancer and the Virologist.
    C. The Drunkard and the Light Machine Gun.
    D. The Factory and the Epileptic.

23. In the third chamber of The Plight House, you find a baby sleeping in a cast-iron cradle. At the centre of the room, a circular trapdoor gapes down onto the darkness of the chamber below. Your task is to drop the baby through the trapdoor. As you lift the child from the cradle, it awakens and gazes at your unfamiliar face. Its eyes are strangely unbeseeching, strangely indifferent to your presence and touch. Which of the following attributes is this chamber designed to test?

    A. Your compassion.
    B. Your cruelty.
    C. Your ability to obey orders.
    D. Your ability to defy orders.

24. You sit down on the floor with the infant cradled hernialike against your body. Falling into a brief and inadvertent sleep, you dream that the chamber below you is occupied by a fairground carousel. The carousel spins wildly out of control, the horses a blur of garish, painted speed. Scattered centrifugal over the surrounding floorboards is a midden of human bones. What is the origin of the carousel's hunger for human flesh?

    A. Vanity: human sacrifice reassures it of its prominence in the dreamlives of men.
    B. Decadence: numb to common pleasures, it has become a devotee of the extreme.
    C. Vengeance: it wishes to punish the children who have abandoned it in favour of more contemporary entertainments.
    D. Vengeance: the horses are real horses, skewered into place by the butchers of yesteryear.

25. The examiner in charge of the third chamber steps forth from his observation post in order to speak with you. He reminds you that you have not yet completed the assigned test. He informs you that the baby has not been chosen randomly. Its future has been foreseen: if allowed to grow up, the child will become a notorious war criminal, slaughtering countless innocents over the course of a long and appalling career. Thanks to which particular aspect of the infant's behaviour do the examiner's words ring true?

    A. The unnerving and sphinxlike stillness of its gaze.
    B. Its failure to register discomfort or pain.
    C. Its failure to cry.
    D. The intensity with which it scratches at your arms and face.

26. Acknowledging your final refusal to complete the test, the examiner summons a nurse from the pediatric ward. As you watch the baby being carried away, you feel with cold and wretched certainty that you have made a terrible mistake. The lights in the chamber begin to fade. The examiner opens the door to the corridor and turns to you with a sad smile. "Come back to us when you're ready," he says. Years from now, when the baby is a grown man, for which of his crimes will you feel the most piercing guilt?

    A. His unprovoked aerial firebombing of a teeming metropolis.
    B. His use of religious cults as a fifth column in low-intensity warfare.

       C. His use of human sacrifices in rituals of the occult.

       D. His clandestine testing of weapons-grade psychoactive agents upon unconsenting civilians.

27. Expelled from The Plight House, you find yourself re-afflicted by the same dark thoughts that drove you to seek treatment. You suffer a complete nervous collapse. Restless and delusional, you begin to hear voices. As you wander aimlessly through the city streets, the voices describe to you a world of delectable sorrow and odd, pernicious wonder. With what aim do they harangue you so incessantly?

       A. To drive you completely, irrevocably insane.

       B. To drive you to commit an act of self-harm.

       C. To drive you back to The Plight House.

       D. To prepare you for the harsher ordeals yet to come.

28. At the age of twenty, in the full grip of your delusions, you imagine yourself to be a sorceress. One day in the marketplace you see a man slap his pregnant wife across the face. As you walk past, you place your hand upon the woman's belly and look into her future. You see that she will die in childbirth and that her husband will be struck blind some five years hence. You utter an imprecation. Which of the following, by dint of your spell, will the unborn child grow to be?

A. A hunchback.
B. An astronaut.
C. A three-legged dog.
D. A swan.

29. At the age of twenty-one, you imagine yourself to be a shape-shifter. In the course of your transmogrifications, you adopt countless forms, both animate and inanimate. One day, after having contorted into the form of a banyan tree, you forget the shape of your own body. What form would you best adopt in order to recall to yourself your natural features?

    A. A key.
    B. A harp.
    C. A human embryo.
    D. A hurricane.

30. You secure employment on the crew of a travelling carnival. You assist in the raising of canvas tents and the assembly of rust-eaten rides. One day, at the height of the season, a young girl falls from the carousel platform and vanishes into the gears below. She dies onsite from her injuries. As the local villagers assemble into a lynchmob, you and your fellow workers strike the carnival and move out under cover of darkness. What do you leave the villagers by way of compensation?

    A. The fortune teller's daughter.
    B. The head of the carousel operator.
    C. A large canvas bag full of mismatched foreign currency.
    D. A clockwork replica of the dead child.

31. I wake up in the morning with a piercing but not unbearable sadness. Call it melancholy. I drink my coffee and gaze out my window into the street below. Outside, people are going to and fro between places I have never seen and on business the nature of which I shall never understand. I envy them their enthusiasm, their sense of purpose. Whence comes gloom of this tenor?

    A. Imbalance of the four humours.
    B. A subtle shift of brain chemistry.
    C. Malnutrition.
    D. Protracted solitude.

32. I receive a telephone call from my ex-wife. She informs me that our daughter has died in an accident at the carnival. My failure to take part in the retributive measures inflicted upon the carnies has been duly noted by the townsfolk and she advises me not to return to the town for our daughter's funeral. With which aspect of my person was my ex-wife most unable to reconcile herself during the seven years of our marriage?

    A. My foreign birth.
    B. My lowly career as a hospital porter.
    C. My prematurely grey hair.
    D. My dislike for her native town.

33. I begin to suffer from insomnia. One night, during a long and footsore walk, I lose my way in an unfamiliar quarter. I consult my map, but every path I take leads me back into the city's darkest and most dangerous sectors. In time, I begin to suspect that my map is intentionally leading me astray. I examine

it carefully until I find, beneath the compass rose, a detail that confirms me in my suspicions. Who is the maker of the map?

    A. The Wander Corporation.
    B. The Human Organ Supply Initiative.
    C. Alzheimer & Son, Cartographers.
    D. Pernicious Game Inc.

34. In the dead of night, unable to sleep, I hear the neighbourhood war-widow singing a lament for her lost love. She is a gifted soprano and her song flows like scented smoke down the deserted city streets. Were I to follow that song to its source and look upon the widow herself, in which of the following would I find her attired?

    A. Her wedding dress.
    B. Funeral black.
    C. Her husband's favourite coat.
    D. Nothing.

35. The war-widow dreams of her husband's death. Her husband is the bombadier on a long-range strategic bomber. Midway through the flight to target, an observer from high command approaches him and stabs him through the neck. The observer then releases the bomber's entire payload onto the allied city below and seats himself at the reticle in order to watch it burn. What force drove the observer to commit this act?

    A. Secret orders from high command.
    B. A deviant sexual drive.
    C. Secret orders from the enemy.
    D. The exhortations of a disembodied voice.

36. I wake up in the morning, my heart so leaden and bereft of fire that I am unable to rise from bed until midday. I prepare my coffee, then leave it on the counter to grow cold. I stare out the window. Afternoon commuters throng the street like dreamless, upright cattle. I hate them. I hate this charnel house of a city and the pointless labours into which we hemorrhage our brief and sombre lives. Whence comes gloom of this tenor?

    A. Protracted solitude.
    B. Cirrhosis of the liver.
    C. Organic brain dementia.
    D. Garden variety urban malaise.

37. You have gone insane. Voices hound you from morning until night and you see the world through the dark and broken matrix of your own confabulations. One day, in the course of rummaging through the trash, you find a fragment of broken concrete wrapped in yellow string. You are convinced that this is a magical object, a sign. What do you interpret it to mean?

    A. "Continue current investigation and maintain course. Help is on the way."
    B. "Meet me tonight in the arboretum. Come alone."
    C. "Danger. Malevolent forces have picked up your trail. Cease all scheduled engagements and go to ground."
    D. "You have failed us for the last time. No child ever squandered so many and such golden opportunities. Speak not when you see us in the street. You are dead to us."

38. There is a knock at your door. Agents from the Department of Squandered Beauty enter your room and begin to search through your belongings. They confiscate all of the fine clothing and jewellery that you have bought but never worn. They confiscate the notebooks into which you have written your ever-unfulfilled plans. And they confiscate your face. You protest that this last requisition is a mistake. What do you offer in support of this protest?

    A. A letter from the head of state, exempting you from such actions.
    B. A box of love letters, each from a different admirer.
    C. A box of love letters, all from the same admirer.
    D. A suicide letter from a rejected admirer.

39. A man drives down a prairie highway at one hundred kilometres an hour. A woman drives toward him at the exact same speed. The man and the woman are counterparts *manqués*: they would fall deeply in love with one another if only fate would bring them together. What do they find at the midpoint of their respective journeys?

    A. A multi-vehicle auto collision in which both of them shall die.
    B. A military transport that has overturned upon the road, its cargo of munitions now laying waste to the surrounding land.
    C. A detour into a land of ordeal where they must either aid one another or perish.
    D. A foundling abandoned upon the road-median.

40. On your twenty-second birthday, as you stand panhandling in the street, a young man approaches and addresses you by name. He is well dressed and handsome, his eyes oddly bright and amethyst in colour. He claims that he knows you, that you and he were childhood friends. You sense that he is sincere in this claim, but, try as you might, you cannot recall ever having met him. The young man asks if you would like to sit and talk over dinner. What is your reply?

   A. "Yes. Though, in truth, I have scant recollection of my childhood and what experiences we might have shared. Tell me more."

   B. "Yes. Though it goes against all my principles to accept the invitation of a stranger, especially one who tells such exquisite lies."

   C. "Yes. Though I resent already your access to my inmost heart. Confess that you will leave me a sadder, more thoroughly broken thing than you found me and I will know you for an honest man."

   D. "No. You have mistaken me for someone else. Leave me alone."

The Plight House

# Section II

1.  You are standing in line outside a healer's tent. It
    is winter. There are hundreds, perhaps thousands,
    of people in line and they keep unwaveringly to
    their places despite the bitter cold. As the line
    inches toward the tent, you notice that each healed
    supplicant bears a freshly-drawn tattoo: an old man
    who had entered the tent confined to a wheelchair
    emerges some five minutes later walking fully
    upright, his neck tattooed with a black spider; a
    blind girl emerges with 20/20 vision and, upon
    her belly, a tattoo of a burning boat. What is your
    ailment? With what figure will the healer mark your
    body and why?

2.  Walking through the ruins of a firebombed city,
    you meet a man dressed in the uniform of a baker.
    He has been disembowelled. He carries his spilled
    intestines before him in a plastic laundry basket
    and around him there has gathered a dense cloud of
    flies. Suffering from shock, he mistakes you for his
    wife and commiserates with you for the destruction
    of your mutual home. He promises to rally help and

construct a new house by winter. He asks what kind of house you would like him to build. What is your reply?

3.  At the age of twenty-three, you marry a tall and handsome foreigner. You are unfamiliar with the customs of his people. On your wedding day, attendants dress you in a skyblue gown and lead you out to the place of union. Sitting upon the altar are a bottle of whisky, thirteen china dogs and a hammer. There is no priest, no presiding official. The groom walks up to the altar and says, "All my wickedness and my roving eye." He then picks up the hammer and smashes one of the china dogs. He drinks. With what oath do you respond? Why is there an odd number of china dogs on the altar?

4.  You secure employment as a private detective. In your first assignment, a large pharmaceutical firm hires you to investigate one of its employees. The individual in question is a member of the janitorial staff and his behaviour has become problematic. He habitually disappears into the corridors of the basement, emerging days later in a besotted, sometimes violent, state. His co-workers are frightened of him. You descend into the bowels of the building, amidst the cables and ductwork, in order to examine the janitor's makeshift quarters. He sleeps in a converted storeroom. It is a squalid place, littered with food tins and dog-eared pornography. On the far wall of the room, hidden behind a curtain, is a door not included in your schematic of the building. By rights, it should open

onto bare bedrock. The door is cold to the touch, the steel deeply etched with a chalkwhite depiction of an apple tree in full bloom. To what place or places does the steel door lead? In what genre of wrongdoing is the janitor engaged?

5. At the age of twenty-five you become pregnant with child. Throughout the first trimester of the pregnancy, you have a recurring dream about a beautiful girl sitting alone on a lakeside dock: as the girl reaches down to touch the water, a hand reaches up and pulls her under. In the second trimester, you dream that the girl emerges from the lake, coughing and sputtering, some two or three hundred metres downshore from the dock; she looks ill and there are strange, runelike blemishes on her once-perfect face. In the third trimester's dream, the girl wanders into the forest and vomits onto the ground a torrent of baby birds. She begins to laugh. What is the dream trying to communicate to you? What will become of the girl after you have given birth to your child?

6. Late at night, while nursing your newborn son, you look out the window and see two men digging a hole in the wasteland beyond your yard. After digging to a depth of some six feet, the men place at the bottom of the hole a briefcase full of money and a leatherbound book. They then fill the hole and depart across the fields. The next morning, you go outside with pick and shovel to exhume the site of the burial. As you begin to dig, you smell strange and exotic perfumes rising from the ground. And

before you reach a depth of even four feet, your shovel strikes wood. It is a trapdoor. What lies beneath the trapdoor? What book must the two men have buried here in order to effect this subterranean transformation?

7. Wandering at leisure in the artisanal quarter, you discover an establishment offering rides on a magic carpet. Curious, you pay your fare and are ushered up a dark and narrow set of stairs to the building's upper floor. The carpet-chamber looks like a hotel room with an old, threadbare carpet in place of a bed. The proprietress tells you that the room is yours for the night. You remove your shoes and lie down on the carpet. You fall asleep and have a vivid dream of flying at exhilarating speed over the surrounding countryside. When you awaken the next morning, you feel reborn: your body is refreshed, your mind quicker and more lucid than it has ever been before. Thenceforward, you visit the establishment three or four times a week. Your nights on the carpet become a passion, then a necessity. You sell off your belongings and move to smaller quarters in order to subsidize your habit. You borrow money from family and friends until they cease to answer your calls. One day you arrive at the establishment to find that the police have conducted a raid and placed the proprietress under arrest. A detective explains to you that the carpet was not magical but rather a commonplace floorcovering soaked with hallucinogenic drugs. Is the detective telling the truth or have the police put forward this explanation in order to keep the carpet for themselves? How do you propose to feed your addiction now?

8.  At the age of twenty-nine, you secure employment as a junior executive in a large investment firm. You develop a particularly close relationship with one of your protégées, a young woman almost ten years your junior. One day you learn from your secretary that your protégée is engaged to be married. You summon the young woman to your office, hinting that you wish to offer your blessings upon the union. Once she is before you, however, you tell her that you have long been sickened by her bad, pitted skin and by the unremitting foulness of her body odour. You accuse her of neglecting herself, of embarrassing the firm with her outmoded and frumpish attire. You terminate her employment. The young woman is devastated by your words and flees the room in tears. The encounter leaves you with a strange, lightheaded sensation, as if you were standing under a shower of anaesthesia. You set a mirror upon the surface of your desk and stare long and hard at your reflection. You take a box-cutter from the desk drawer and slash your cheek from temple to jawline, the blade biting all the way down to bone. Still you feel nothing. What is the cause of this sudden, all-consuming numbness? How might you recover the capacity for sensation and what are the potential drawbacks of such a recovery?

9.  Your eldest son is a sullen, joyless child. By the age of eight, he has a vicious temper and a cold, unflinching stare. He swears like a convict. He spends hours on end drawing dense and strangely violentlooking pictures, his face clenched all the while in an expression of bitter discontent. You

appeal to your husband to take the situation in hand, but he believes the boy's behaviour to be normal, the stuff of a strong, if brooding, masculinity. One day, you receive a call from the police. They have placed your son in custody following an incident in the schoolyard. Your son, having received a love letter from a girl in his class, reciprocated by handing the girl a lighter and a bottle of gasoline. He then told her that he would love her forever if she set herself on fire. The girl accepted his gambit and now lies in hospital, only barely clinging to life. Preliminary testing indicates that your son had altered the gasoline with some kind of gelatin, in the manner of napalm, with the intention of increasing its destructive power. What is wrong with your son? In what ways will you treat or regard him differently when he is released back into your care?

10. You awaken in the night, seized with the sudden conviction that an object of great value has gone missing from your home. In a kind of methodical frenzy, you run through the house emptying every cupboard and every drawer. You drag from your closet boxes that have not seen light for years and pour their contents pell-mell onto the floor. Your search grows more desperate as the night wears on. Your rummagings awaken your husband and children and they watch in horror as you sift like a madwoman through your spilled impedimenta. By daybreak, you still have not found the object for which you are searching. You have, however, found three objects for whose presence you cannot account: a compass, a map and a key. What person

or persons sequestered these items in the crannies of your home? Why at this particular juncture are you being called forth to a journey?

11. In the weeks leading up to your thirty-second birthday, you notice a degradation in the quality of your memory. The lapses are not serious in themselves—a lost garment here, a misplaced document there—but, concerned nonetheless, you seek medical attention. Your family physician informs you that you have developed a rare and serious form of galloping amnesia, the progression of which will in short order wipe your mind completely, irrevocably blank. Within a matter of months you will lose even your grasp of human speech and thereby become a stranger in every land. Leaving the doctor's office, you realize that you have forgotten the make and model of your car. The sensation of forgetting is strangely pleasureable, the cognitive equivalent of removing a pair of heavy boots. Moreover, it has transformed the simple matter of finding your car into a kind of quest or game. Will you apprise your husband of the doctor's diagnosis or will you keep it to yourself, a secret? Why does the impending erasure of your mind feel less like a death sentence, more like the return of an old and loyal friend?

12. One bright morning you sit up in bed to find a strange man lying beside you. Frightened, you extricate yourself from beneath the bedcovers and steal from the room. As you go to call for help, you find that several other rooms in your home have likewise been requisitioned by strangers. Two young

boys are sleeping in the guest room and there is a girl in the study. The furnishings with which you had decorated said rooms are gone and the intruders have filled them instead with clothing and toys and child-sized furniture of their own. Whilst you wander the house, taking stock of the changes that have been wrought upon it, the intruders awaken and crowd about you. The children wish you a happy birthday. The man proffers to you a giftbox wrapped in fine paper and ribbons. You run from the house. Who are these intruders and how will you dislodge them from your home? Where will you take shelter in the meantime?

13. You wander the hinterlands north of the city. Besides the slippers on your feet and the clothing on your back, your only material possessions are your recently-discovered compass, map and key. A crimson X on the map marks what you presume to be your destination and you navigate your way toward it over three cold autumn days and nights. It is not until you emerge from the forest path and find yourself standing at the edge of the quarry that you realize you are returning to The Plight House. The weather in this region has been dry all year and this time there is no floodwater to interfere with your arrival: you reach the quarry floor by descending the ramps that curve threadlike down its walls. The door to The Plight House is weatherbeaten oak and your key turns easily in the lock. Once inside the facility, you surrender to your exhaustion, lying down on the floor in a position of graceless repose. From the depths of your slumber, you perceive the approach

of distant lights and voices. Do you believe yourself to be better able to pass the tests now than you were on your first attempt more than a decade ago? Why or why not? In what respects can your nervous collapse and your years of humble drudgery be considered a form of training for this second all-important attempt?

14. You awaken in a cramped one-room apartment under the rafters of The Plight House. The bed in which you lie smells of dampness and sweat. Stretched out on the floor beside you is the examiner who, fourteen years ago, expelled you from the facility. He sits up slowly from a stiffnecked sleep and apologizes for the cramped accommodations. Over a simple meal of porridge and coffee, the examiner warns you that the hardships you will face in the chambers ahead will be crueller and more protracted than the ones you remember, since the facility will take full advantage of your established vulnerabilities. After breakfast, as he prepares to go to work, the examiner ventures to ask if you feel ready to resume your place in the battery of tests. "Not quite yet," you reply. You spend the day alone in the examiner's room, drinking tea and dozing and pacing the meagre floorspace. Is it possible to gain some insight into the methods of The Plight House by studying the examiner's papers and personal effects? Are you shocked by the squalor in which the examiner lives and what, by contrast, did you expect?

15. Over the weeks to follow, you constantly put off your return to the battery, complaining of fatigue and headache. Gradually, you and the examiner fall into a lukewarm domesticity. The two of you make small talk over meals and chores and even share the narrow bed. Not that there is a romantic component. At night you sleep side by side like things unsexed, muttering apologies when you touch. Whenever you so much as remove a sweater, the examiner turns away as if struck. From this and other clues, you build a picture of a man who has acquiesced to the cancer of celibacy. At times you find his manner unaccountably frustrating. He acts like an old man though your conversations have revealed that he is but four years your senior. He repeats himself. He carps and he cavils. Every second or third evening, he lectures you about the need to reclaim your original ardour and throw yourself back into the battery. Sometimes you respond with a half-hearted promise. Other times you abandon him outright, leaving the room without fanfare and going for a stroll through the barracks. The examiners whom you meet on the gangways and stairs observe you with knowing smiles, your bedmate not the first among them to have plucked a mistress from the flock. What field or fields must the prospective examiner study in order to secure employment at The Plight House? Or is qualification a matter of rejecting established fields and how, then, is the force of that rejection gauged?

16. One day the examiner fails to come home from work. His clothes and belongings still lie scattered around the room, so you presume that he will soon return. As his absence extends to a second and third day, however, you begin to fear for his well-being. On the eleventh day after his disappearance, you receive a letter. In it, the examiner explains that he has resigned his post and departed The Plight House forever. He apologizes for having tried to hasten your return to the battery, admitting that he was wrong to have done so. The entire purpose of The Plight House is to inflict upon test subjects the exact ordeals they lack the fortitude to inflict upon themselves. His exhortations were therefore the very height of absurdity and he asks your forgiveness for having uttered them. He informs you that, by way of recompense, he has secured your permanent release from testing and that you may stay in his room for as long as you like. He bids you farewell. Over the years to follow, you receive a number of such letters from the examiner, each one postmarked from a different far-flung locale. His anecdotes leave you with the distinct impression that he leads something of an itinerant life. He writes about hitchhiking and odd forms of day-labour, about nights spent at fireside with his fellow wayfarers. In his final letter, written more than five years after his original disappearance, he shares with you his longheld dream of fleeing to the distant mountains and becoming a solitary woodsman. By the simple rhythm of cutting wood and burning it, sleeping and waking, he will lull his life through to an unthrilling close. What compensation was the examiner obliged to offer in

exchange for your removal from the battery? How does this compensation relate to his desire to live a life of utter solitude?

17. After the examiner's departure, you live a quiet, near-invisible life in your room beneath the rafters. The examiner has diverted to you his pension and uncollected backpay so that you are able to purchase goods from the commissary. You while away the days. You take long, aimless walks through the depths of The Plight House and spend entire afternoons hibernating in bed. One day, in the course of your wanderings, you see that the door to the third chamber has been left open. You step inside. The chamber looks exactly the way you remember it— the cast-iron cradle, the circular trapdoor—even if the baby in the cradle is now a different one. Looking around the room with older, jaded eyes, you find the test to be almost preposterously simple. And you laugh at yourself for having missed the answer before. You leave the baby in its cradle—for it is, you now understand, nothing but a distraction—and walk up to the edge of the trapdoor. You peer down once into the lightless depths, then allow yourself to fall. The darkness accepts you like an old lover. In the thrill of your descent, you recall your long-forgotten childhood vow that you would always be a voluptuary, that you would cherish above all other things that which is pure and extreme. Now indeed is the time to reclaim old hungers. With this fall, you have cast off the rags of sobriety and pledged your body a repository for rare and overwhelming

sensations. At what point in your life did you lose your hunger for pure and extreme sensation? How will its return help you to prevail in ordeals where the will to self-preservation is a guarantor of failure?

18. On my first night away from The Plight House, I have a dream in which you figure prominently. In the dream, we hold a long and intimate conversation while wandering down the halls of a crumbling, labyrinthine mansion. We talk about music and childhood and highways and the sea. We talk about our shared fear of growing old and rotting away in solitude. Eventually, we become separated and you find yourself alone in the attic, surrounded by old brushes and half-used cans of paint. Like all dreamers, I have a terrible memory. What could you write or draw upon the walls to recall to me our conversation and the bewitching interlocutrix that you are?

19. I join a travelling sideshow. I specialize in performing auto-impalement with icepicks and needles and knives. After travelling with the sideshow for three consecutive seasons, I become bored with the life of the performer. I grow ashamed of my poverty. And I come to despise, more than I had ever thought possible, the nightly throngs of awestruck simpletons whose distraction is my livelihood. One day I receive an invitation to a seminar by a local doctor of the healing arts. The doctor bears numerous esoteric credentials and claims that he can awaken even the most jaded senses, the deadest

of dreams. To me, this seems an unlikely prospect. Describe an act that the doctor could perform which would indeed restore to me my old sense of wonder.

20. I construct a sensory deprivation chamber. I fill the chamber with heated salt water and seal myself inside. Even after eight hours of immersion, however, I experience none of the chamber's purported effects: no sense of disembodiment, no visual or auditory hallucinations. Frustrated, I cut short the session. I open the lid of the chamber and sit upright, only to find that I am no longer in my home. My contraption sits like a matchbox in the middle of a vast and featureless room. The room has no doors and no windows, the only light coming from a circular hatch in the ceiling, some eight or nine metres overhead. Where am I? How did I transport myself to this place and what must I do in order to return home?

21. My mother has fallen ill. Her condition is deteriorating rapidly and her doctors have told me to abandon all hope that she will recover. Whilst attending to her needs, I find beneath her bed a cast-iron statuette depicting a pig with seven eyes. I ask my mother how this object came to be in her bedroom, but she has no explanation. I remove the statuette from the house and throw it in the garbage. Upon my next visit, however, I find beneath her bed either the very same object or some new and identical facsimile. What is the statuette's connection to my mother's illness and why can I not

dispose of it in the conventional manner? What is the occult significance of the seven-eyed pig?

22. I find work in a slaughterhouse. I perfect the techniques of killing with blade and boltgun alike and soon I can dress a fresh carcass faster than any of my peers. In a bid to outmanoeuvre the slaughterhouse's competition, management begins to purchase a new kind of livestock. The animals in question are small, doglike creatures with tawny hair and wide, nocturnal eyes. Management warns us to wear earplugs whilst slaughtering them, as their song has been known to unhinge the human mind. From the moment that I start practicing my trade upon these creatures, I begin to suffer from terrible nightmares. My nights become a hell of strange and vivid horrors and within three weeks' time I am legless with fatigue. One day, acting on a sudden and uncharacteristic impulse, I rescue one of the creatures from the killing-room floor and hide it in my coveralls. I bring it home. Sitting on my kitchen table, scanning the room with its dark eyes, the creature looks innocuous and unafraid. I remove my earplugs. What does the creature say to me?

23. I reach the age of forty without having found a mate. Just as my prospects run dry for what I fear is the last time, I receive a telephone call. A woman with a beautiful voice is responding to a personal advertisement that I had placed more than a year earlier. She invites me to join her for a late supper. As

I arrive at her apartment, flowers in hand, the door opens of its own accord. I look inside. Rats move to and fro along the baseboards and the floor is littered with empty liquor bottles. The air reeks of ashtrays, urine and fear. The beautiful voice calls out to me from somewhere inside the apartment. What fate has befallen all previous callers to this place? Why do I step inside nonetheless?

24. I am attending the funeral of a fellow examiner who has died young. Among the mourners is a stranger. The stranger is tall and cadaverously thin, with piercing, intelligent eyes. He is disruptive throughout the service, nodding sycophantically during the eulogy and singing the hymns in a tremendous baritone that clears the pews before him like a watercannon. After the service, as we file from the church, he takes the dead man's mother by the hand. "Your son is a dullard of the highest order," he says. "You can have him back." I turn to face the altar and see that the casket is empty, its former occupant now shuffling dazedly up the aisle. Who is the stranger with the piercing, intelligent eyes? By what agency has he resurrected my old colleague and what does he ask in return?

25. I marry. I father children and work tirelessly to provide for them. One day, while dining with my family, I rise from the table and walk out the door. I walk briskly up the street, away from the harbour and the towers of the financial district. As darkness falls, I reach the city limits and press onward into

the countryside, the din of suburban lights and lawns fading echolike behind me. I walk for days and weeks. My appearance grows haggard and unkempt and my clothes turn to rags upon my withered frame. As my fugue extends into the winter months, I enter the lake-riddled district far to the north of the city. On a cold and cloudless night, I see a carnival train parked at the side of the road. The carnies have uncoupled the carousel from the train and are pushing it out onto a frozen lake. They tell me that the carousel is cursed. They tell me that they are leaving it on the ice so that the spring thaw may consign it to the lakebottom forever. As I take my leave of the carnies and continue my trek northward, I feel a monumental relief to be once again alone. My aversion to human company has bloomed into a deep and violent loathing. What is the origin of my thirst for perdition and why is walking a means to achieve it? How will I know when I have reached my destination?

The Plight House

# Section III

1.   You are the madam of a large and profitable brothel. Your clientele includes many of the city's artistic luminaries and some of its most powerful financiers. One night you hear a commotion in the upper bedchambers. You go upstairs and find a crowd gathered outside the executive suite. The guard on duty informs you that one of your whores has been brutally assaulted with a butcherknife. As you enter the room, you see that the victim is one of your youngest and most comely acquisitions. Her eyes are agape and fixed on the ceiling. Her breath is shallow. You tell her to describe the man who attacked her. "He was beautiful," she says. Seconds later, she dies.

1a.   You assemble your lackeys in the parlour. Some of them are armed with knives, some with pistols. You yourself are armed with both. All of you are dressed in your best black finery and the brothel's photographer marks the occasion by taking a group portrait. Before setting out, you treat your lackeys to a great feast. With what dishes and delicacies do you furnish their table? Do you discourage the consumption of alcohol in light of the work that lies ahead? Why or why not?

1b. You fan out into the ghetto in threes and fours, interrogating the local inhabitants and shopkeepers for information. Fear of the killer, however, is both more widespread and more intense than you had anticipated, silencing even your most dependable informants. What, then, is a suitable level of force to employ in the course of these interrogations? How would you describe the regard in which you are held throughout the district and how can you best employ this reputation to your advantage?

1c. You visit the other brothels in the quarter and ask if they have had any unusually violent customers. The madam of a brothel called the Ocean House says that a man came to her door earlier in the week asking which of the local establishments was yours. He referred to you by name. You ask her to describe the man and she replies, "He was beautiful." To what specific sexual fetish does the Ocean House cater? In what respects might running a brothel of this kind be preferable to running one that services a general clientele?

1d. Your lackeys report that they have heard rumours of a strange man staying at the central hotel. According to witnesses, the man is tall and thin and immaculately dressed. All of them remark upon his unusual eyes, which are the colour and brightness of amethyst. You go immediately to the hotel, but the man has departed. Scanning the ledger, you see that he had signed in under the name "the Prettymaker." Why do your men shudder at the mention of this name when you, yourself, do not? What name would the murderer have best chosen in order to strike fear into your heart?

1e. The hotel bartender provides additional information. The Prettymaker had stayed at the hotel for a week all told and each night he spent long hours drinking at the bar. He spoke of you constantly and he spoke of you with bitterness. He claimed that you and he were one another's first love, as children. Having recently made his fortune, he had set out in order to find you and ask your hand in marriage. He claimed to have been devastated by the discovery that you had become a flesh-peddler, a base procuress of women and children. His love then souring overnight into a monomaniacal hatred, he swore vengeance upon you. By what name did you know the Prettymaker in the days of your youth? Did he exhibit even then a predilection for savagery? Why should the mere discovery of your profession act as the stressor for his current psychosexual rampage?

1f. You devise a stratagem. You send home all your assorted henchmen and sequester your whores in a resort by the sea. You open every window and every door in the brothel. Once having completed these steps, you go up to the executive suite, strip naked and go to sleep in the dead girl's bed. The Prettymaker comes to you in the dead of night. You can feel his presence even across the partitions of slumber, for his anger warps the darkness like a bombcrater at your bedside. He radiates the sheer, unutterable hurt of having lost you not to death or distance or any of the common vicissitudes but, rather, to the joyless blood-wealth of the sextrade. And the sight of your naked body fills him with pain. In the morning, you awaken to find the Prettymaker hanging from the rafters, a makeshift noose around his beautiful neck. He is dead. When the drunks and whoremongers of the future convene in their dives, how will they speak of your victory over the Prettymaker? What embellishments and omissions will they make? What are your feelings as you look upon the corpse of your first love, and does the sight of him recall to you in any measure the love you once shared?

2.  You have amnesia. Mute and penniless, you wander the streets of a great metropolis, surviving various dark and violent encounters with the predators of the urban night. Eventually, you are taken in by a community of the homeless. You live with these newfound friends in a shantytown by the railyards, scavenging your sustenance from out of the city's garbage. Years pass. One night you have a vivid

dream about a quiet house in the suburbs. The house is clean and bright, with herringbone floors and a spicegarden beneath the kitchen window. You awaken from the dream with a deep and heartfelt conviction that the house will be yours if only you step forth and claim it. You can even remember the address.

2a. You go to the house and ring the doorbell. A man answers the door. He is about to ask you your business when his expression transforms into a look of profound shock. This man is your husband. Seventeen years ago, on your birthday, you walked away from the family home, never to be seen again. You have been listed as a missing person ever since. What does your husband believe to have been the reason for your departure? Did the detectives who investigated your disappearance concur with him in this regard? How many lovers has your husband taken in the years since you left?

2b. Overjoyed by your sudden, unexpected return, your husband takes you on a tour of the house. He recounts for you the provenance of new furnishings he has purchased since your children fled the nest. The decor, he tells you, looks much the way it did when you left, for he had not the heart to change it. And, in truth, he had never stopped hoping for your return. Is there any material thing for which you have longed over the years? A favourite book? A dress? Or do these objects carry some dark import even now and do you avert your eyes, repelled?

2c. Seven days after your arrival, you have still not spoken aloud. Your husband believes your silence to be the result of some trauma suffered during the years of your absence. And though he craves to hear your voice, he is careful not to pressure you into speaking. He clings to the belief that given time you will regain your powers of speech, whatever doubts have now begun to assail him. What, indeed, are the statistical chances that your silence can be overcome? Can you compensate for it by engaging in some alternate form of communication, like writing or drawing pictures?

2d. Over the weeks that follow, you remain uncommunicative. Fearing that his presence is exacerbating your condition, your husband retreats into a parallel solitude. The situation has become difficult for him to bear. The original hurt of losing you has returned to him twofold, its virulence enhanced by dark and recriminatory images of your suffering. Wracked with guilt, he hides in his study night after night, looking at old photo albums and drinking himself into a stupor. He thrashes in his sleep as if bodily confronting the demons that drove you from his side. Why have you returned if not so that you and your husband might reclaim the contentment you once shared? Is your return an act of retribution and, if so, for what are you taking vengeance?

2e. Three months after your return, your husband has become a paragon of self-neglect. Bearded and filthy, he lives in a state of almost perpetual drunkenness. One grey morning he dresses in his warmest clothes and fills a pack with provisions. He leaves the house. He makes his way down into the shatteredmost sector of the inner city and there constructs a shelter out of sheetmetal and stray boards. After days of unremitting inebriation, he is inspired to commit an act of self-harm. He sharpens his scissors. Once both the blades are razor-keen, he hacks off his tongue at the root and throws it like afterbirth into the canal. Has your husband left the house because he regards your marriage as defunct? Or do his actions, to the contrary, indicate a renewed commitment to his vows? How long and how harsh an ordeal will he have to undergo in order to become once again your perfect counterpart?

3. I have fallen ill. The sickness that I have contracted is a rare and unstudied disease. The doctors have placed me in isolation against the possibility of contagion and ordered that all nursing staff wear gloves and mask in my presence. As my condition deteriorates, my mind floats wildly adrift. Bouts of high fever leave me dazed and frail and, in my delirium, I begin to have a succession of ever darker and ever more erotic dreams. Dreams of bodies thrilled and broken. Of ropes and teeth and fire. The nurses recount to me an unusual phenomenon: when I wake up in the morning, after dreaming

thus, my eyes are not their natural brown colour but a strange, ferocious amber.

3a. The fever breaks. I sit up in bed and begin to talk incessantly. The words pour relentlessly from my mouth, as if I had become a medium for some lost and restive spirit. I repeat over and over that I must leave the hospital and find my way back to my beloved, for her company alone will restore me to health. The doctors ask me for my beloved's name and address, but I find myself unable to recall either piece of information. Why do I not know the details most pertinent to the fulfillment of my stated quest? What is the conventional relationship between a quest's level of difficulty and the intrinsic value of its objective? How does that relationship bear upon my current situation?

3b. Fearing that I will talk myself into a state of exhaustion, the doctors inject me with a sedative. I fall asleep. In the bleak and chemical dreams that follow, I imagine that my body has been drained of all blood, my vascular system filled instead with a mercury-coloured, molten metal. Looking at myself in the mirror, I see that beneath my skin the once blue deltawork of veins is now grey and slightly luminous. The strangeness of this new body makes me feel potent and otherwordly, like some creature unleashed from the realms of darkest fairytale, but at the same time I fear that I have become hideous in the eyes of womankind. Given the nature of my physical transformation, what percentage of women will henceforward find me less attractive and what percentage more? Of those who find me more attractive, what percentage will have experimented with body modification and/or self-mutilation involving a metal implement?

3c. I awaken from my period of sedation afflicted with a severe stomach ache. A dazzling, whitehot pain crawls upward through my lower abdomen like a wandering fragment of shrapnel. I curl into the foetal position. The pain intensifies with the passing of the hours and, as darkness falls, it begins to migrate up my throat. Late at night, I lean over the side of the bed and vomit onto the linoleum a black and placentalike heap of gore. The heap scurries away from me and hides in a corner of the room. Of what biological order is this abomination? What would have been the consequences of having held it within my body?

3d. Over the days that follow, the abomination grows larger and larger. The doctors and nurses come and go without seeing it, as if it were cohering on a wavelength visible to me alone. After three days, the abomination begins to sing. After five days, it stands like a deranged boychild of six or seven years and strides over to my bedside. It tells me that it has come here to guide me back to my beloved. It tells me to rise from my bed. How do I know that the abomination is not trying to deceive me? What song did it sing in the final days of its quickening and what meaning should I read into this choice of music?

3e. The abomination leads me down into the hospital basement and together we enter a maze of corridors and stairwells. After a half day's journey, it is clear that we have strayed beyond the precincts of the hospital and crossed into some greater subterranean ductwork. We walk for three days and three nights. Our journey ends at the door to a giant incinerator. The abomination opens the incinerator door and climbs inside, beckoning me to follow. Hesitant, I reach my hand into the flames. My skin smoulders and blisters and burns, but I feel no pain. My sickness has rendered me insensate to fire. Who is my beloved? Where did we first meet? What name shall science bestow upon the illness that has reunited us at last?

4. Your son and daughter-in-law have gone on vacation, leaving their nine-year-old daughter in your care. She is your only grandchild. She is articulate and highly intelligent, but there is much in her demeanour that causes you concern. She is too quiet, too serious. She would rather sit alone with her books and dolls than go outside to meet with playmates. In an effort to dispel her habitual gloom, you take her to the annual autumn fair. As you walk with her amongst the stalls and coloured balloons, you offer to buy candy floss and to let her play a game on the midway. She declines on both counts. You offer to

buy her a turn on the rides, but she complains that they look unsafe. After an hour of being rebuffed, you decide that this is a wasted outing. Your path back to the gate takes you past the fair's haunted house. The haunted house is a dilapidated structure, muralled with lurid images of axe-murderers and ghouls. As you walk past, your granddaughter slows, enraptured by the howling and screams within. It is clear from the intensity of her gaze that she wishes to go inside. Eager that she should enjoy at least one of the fair's attractions, you buy the requisite ticket. She thanks you and rushes over to take her place in line. Such a morbid child.

4a. Your granddaughter sits in a rickety black fun-house car. As the car lurches forward into the darkness, she turns toward you and waves. She is smiling. You wait for her at the exit, resolving that you will not quibble about the price of a second ticket if she wishes to take the ride again. Eventually, however, you realize that your granddaughter has been inside the haunted house for too long. All of the patrons who entered it after her have long since emerged from within. You go to the head of the line to seek assistance, but the ticket-taker has vanished, the entrance to the ride now boarded up and locked. What is your darkest fear regarding your granddaughter's failure to appear at the exit? What is the likelihood that something of a dark and terrible nature has indeed come to pass, as opposed to there being a more mundane explanation?

4b. You search the fair for someone who can help you, but no one is interested in your predicament. You leave the fair and go to the police. You tell your story to the constable on duty and, though he seems not to share your sense of urgency, he agrees to drive you back to the fair. He parks his cruiser on the service road and you lead him on foot up the hill that overlooks the fairground. As you crest the hill, however, and the vista unfolds before you, you see that the fair is gone. In its place is a vast and sordid scrap yard. Heaps of carhulks and broken machinery cover the ground as far as the eye can see. As you stand there agape, the constable tells you that there is nothing of which to be ashamed, that it is commonplace for persons of your age to become confused from time to time. He offers to drive you home. What has happened to the fair? From where has all this scrapmetal come and how did it overwhelm the fairground in the brief span of your absence?

4c. You take your leave of the constable and go wandering through the scrap. You search for several hours without finding any sign of your granddaughter. You have begun to despair of ever seeing her again when, finally, at the far edge of the site, you find an old, battered shipping container. The container is obscured by the detritus shored up against its hull, but you can discern that it is of similar shape and dimension to the fair's haunted house. Stepping into the container's maw, you find the interior to be strangely rustless and clean. Partitions of corrugated steel have been upreared against the light, like the walls of a maze, and you must wend your way through them in order to proceed forward. In the pitch dark of the container's nether side, you find a spiral staircase leading down through the floor. Under ideal conditions, what provisions would you have upon your person as you descend the spiral stair? Are you a seasoned explorer of bunkers and caves? What are some of the challenges unique to subterranean navigation and how do you propose to tackle them unequipped?

4d. The staircase leads you down two or perhaps three storeys, depositing you at its terminus at the entrance to an underground tunnel. A dim and crepuscular light emanates from the bare rock walls, like the discharge from buried phosphorus. The tunnel is perhaps thrice the girth of the container above. It is home to a subterranean apple orchard. The trees, planted gridform in the subterranean soil, bear a lush but sicklooking foliage that prevents you from seeing more than a few short metres down the tunnel. The apples that hang from the treebranches are ivory in colour and have an unappealing, waxy texture. Having set foot in this venue, you feel an immediate rush of certainty that your granddaughter is somewhere nearby. Do you believe her to have been brought here against her will or has she simply become lost in the course of some ill-conceived adventure of her own device? What dangers and perils prevent her from escaping without your aid?

4e. You go wandering into the orchard, hoping to establish its limits and thereby delineate the scope of your search. But the tunnel is prodigiously long. You walk down its length for what you estimate to be at least two hours without seeing any sign of either the tunnel's end or your granddaughter. Tired and crestfallen, you sit down at the base of a tree. You pick up from the ground one of the strange, subterranean apples and bite into it. The flesh is sickly sweet and fills your belly with a brandylike warmth. You curl up on the ground and fall asleep. How long do you believe yourself to be asleep and how long is your sleep in actuality? Do you fight all the while to rouse yourself or is the lure of slumber too powerful, too strong?

4f. You awaken to find that whilst you slept your body has been rejuvenated to that of a twenty-year-old. Your skin is tight and unwrinkled. You are fecund. The light in the orchard is brighter now and you can see that you had fallen asleep within shouting distance of the tunnel's end. Down through the trees, the walls open trumpetlike on a vast subterranean hillscape, the orchard transforming beyond that point into a dark and tangled forest. Mineral pockets wink in the ceiling like toy metallic stars. You begin to weep. Why? What lies in the wilds beyond the orchard? What will become of your newly-regained youth if you stray from this place and can this end be in no way forestalled?

5. I am a soldier. In recognition of my long and distinguished career, I have been appointed commanding officer of a newly-formed regiment within the branch for psychological warfare. My mandate is to develop special techniques for sowing fear and terror in the enemy. For the purposes of starting up the unit, I have been given free rein to recruit directly out of the civilian population. In this, I gravitate immediately toward the demimonde. Down in the asylums and the rooming-houses of our cities, I meet with scientists who have been blacklisted for conducting dark and unorthodox forms of experimentation. I call back from exile old spymasters known for their ferocity and lack of scruple. In introducing myself to these recruits, I promise to provide them not only with handsome remuneration but also with a milieu untouched by the burdens of civilian constraint. As members of my regiment, they will join an elite fellowship of unconventional minds. Where others might offer mere employment and lodging, I offer a vocation and a home.

5a. The first phase of our research focuses upon the manipulation of unconventional religious groups. The most promising prospect unearthed by our research is a cult that calls itself the Voice of the Worm. The members of this cult adhere to a heterodox belief system that values ugliness over beauty, their cosmos being presided over by a pair of deformed identical twins who favour the physically wretched in all things. The cult's doctrine of hostility toward the conventional human form makes its members ideal for carrying out violent, high-impact operations against a wide variety of targets. I begin the task of arming the group and providing its members with basic paramilitary training. I place the cult's leader on payroll. Oversight committee, however, fails to approve the final stages of the plan's implementation. What are some of the potential benefits and drawbacks, tactically speaking, of using such a group against an enemy population? What are some of the potential benefits and drawbacks of using it against a friendly population?

5b.  The second phase of our research focuses upon the occult. After assembling a collection of notorious grimoires, we set about summoning a host of the greater demons. The demons with whom we make contact have vast, unspeakable powers. With a mere snap of the fingers, they can paralyze an entire brigade. But the price of their compacts is steep and most often payable in blood alone. A simple spell of disorientation might require the sacrifice of thirty children. We try for a time to fulfill these demands, but in the end it is simply beyond our logistical means to pursue this line of research. Had this phase borne fruit, how should I have presented it to the oversight committee? What would have been their probable reaction to the necessity of blood sacrifice and how could I have framed it in order to make it more palatable?

5c. Our third research phase is devoted to hallucinogenics. It is an approach that pays immediate dividends since mere microns of a carefully engineered compound can incapacitate an enemy combatant for hours. We assemble an extensive battery of drugs, each one designed to induce a different kind of dementia. We develop advanced systems of payload delivery. And throughout our research, we release small amounts of our compounds to local dealers of illegal narcotics for distribution in recreational channels. As such, we are able to present our work to the oversight committee as a form of reciprocity, a refinement of techniques already being used against our population by an unknown, unseen enemy. Oversight, in turn, approves our research for use in the field. For what kinds of use should we earmark funds gained from extra-legal sales of our compounds? How best to collect data on short- and long-term effects from the ranks of civilian addicts?

5d. The first field use of our work is a resounding success. Commanders of an expeditionary force fire a dose of compound E-019 at an entrenched enemy position. Scores of enemy combatants come wandering out of their bunkers, dazed and unarmed, as if some latterday game of hide-and-seek had come to an end. A simple barrage of anti-personnel ordnance then cuts them to pieces. Our unit receives a commendation, plus additional funding and manpower. What portion of these new resources should I devote to the continuation of phase three operations and what portion to new research? Should I now re-consider presenting phase two (occult) to the oversight committee, given the reputation for success that the unit now enjoys? Why or why not?

5e. The weeks that follow are a blur of dinners and congratulatory handshakes. Morale in the unit is high. One day, during an early morning trip to the firing range, I experience a distinct hypervivid sensation. My mind races. The colours of the morning turn bright and surreal and I feel as if I could count the leaves on every distant tree. On the firing range itself, my aim is uncannily true and with minimal effort I achieve the scores of an expert marksman. After the session, I disassemble and clean my weapon. The course of reassembly, however, takes longer than usual and, once having completed it, I find that the weapon is much larger than it was before. Fell and unwieldy like a truck-mounted cannon, it is now too heavy for me to carry. In submitting the weapon for replacement or repair, how should I describe the defect that afflicts it? How best to convey my unequivocal certainty that the problem is one of workmanship and not botched reassembly?

5f. I return to headquarters to find the sentry hut
unmanned and the sound of live fire crackling
in the distance. Members of the regiment
are combing the grounds in full battle gear,
conducting what appears to be some kind
of intense but poorly coordinated search.
I stop a passing soldier and order him to brief
me on the situation. He says that the men are
conducting a treasure hunt. He says that the
quartermaster has already found a fifteen-year
vintage of Brilliant Apple Wine. I go to the
quartermaster's office and find him sitting on
the floor, a bottle of silver fluid cradled in his lap.
I ask him why no one informed me of the hunt.
By way of answer, he opens his mouth in a huge
and silent yawn: a light brighter than the sun
pours firelike from his gullet. What are some
of the other treasures being contested in the
hunt? Should I, having arrived late on the scene,
content myself with amassing a collection of
minor objects? Or should I risk all and devote
myself wholeheartedly to the pursuit of one of
the major treasures?

5g. I join the hunt. My search leads me away
from the main compound and into the forest.
Darkness falls. The forest draws me down
crooked byways deeper and deeper into its core,
like a labyrinth of roots and branches. In time,
I come to a clearing where a short and silver
grass grows hairlike under the moon. Standing
in the center of the clearing is my first love. She
has not aged and she is dressed exactly as

she was the day I left her. I step into the clearing, but she runs away. I try to pursue her, but when I reach the place where she was standing, I find lying in the grass a freshly eviscerated human heart. Curious, I reach into my shirt. My fingers pass blindly through a wet and boneless incision and into the darkness of my chest cavity. As I grope like an organthief through the folds of my body, I hear the roar of fighter planes overhead. I hear a series of loud explosions as bombs rain down onto headquarters. How did my first love come to be in this place, on this particular night? Why does she flee from me? Which of my enemies is attacking headquarters and to whom should I go for help?

6. You are an astronaut-in-training. Years of study and physical conditioning have secured for you a place among the space program's elite. Thus far in your training, you have been ranked ahead of almost all your peers. So long as you maintain this level of performance, it is only a matter of time before you are selected for a spacemission. One day, during a routine transoceanic flight, your training jet experiences a catastrophic electrical malfunction. You are unable to restore power and the plane crashes into the sea. You lose consciousness. Upon awakening, you find yourself marooned on a tropical island. The island is a paradisiacal setting. Fruit trees grow in abundance throughout the lush interior and the lagoon is teeming with fish. A network of mountainside caverns and caves offers shelter from the elements. In short, the

island provides for all your fundamental needs and there is no reason to believe that you could not survive here for months, even years, whilst you await help.

6a. Working on the assumption that you will be rescued shortly, you take great pains to protect your acuity of mind. You know that your standing in the space program hinges upon your ability to do so. You write equations and formulae in the sand in order to retain your command of physics and mathematics. You recite detailed articles of procedure that you have committed verbatim to memory. In the end, however, after many long months of solitude, you are unable to stave off the onset of isolation sickness. You grow weary and mournful, your senses deprived of stimuli. You wander the beach for hours at a time, longing to be touched or to look upon another human being. As the sickness worsens, you begin to forget the faces of your family and friends. In what manner do their features disband? Who is the first to be forgotten and who the last?

6b. Time passes. You spend the evenings singing pop songs and commercial jingles. It is a practice that, initially, gives you great pleasure. Certain portions of song lyric have dropped from your memory, but this is no great matter: you make up lyrics of your own to bridge the gaps and thereby maintain the songs' continuity. One night, however, as you go through your repetoire, you realize that you are singing lyrics comprised almost entirely of your own improvisations. And soon thereafter you forget all fragment of the originals. It is around this time that you acquire the habit of soliloquy. On what subjects are you most fond of speaking? Who are your interlocutors? Are their identities fixed and stable or do they shift like figures in a dream?

6c. Time passes. One day, while bathing in the stream, you are struck with the distinct impression that you are being watched. You dress yourself hurriedly and flee back to your cave. You calm yourself by reasoning that your fear is without basis, for you have seen no footprints, no indication of another person living on the island. The next morning, however, as you look down onto the beach, you see that a message has been written in the sand. It reads, "You are mine." Describe the style of script. Is it brutal and childish or does it convey a sinister elegance? What are your feelings as you read this message? What, if anything, is your response?

6d. It is the island, you realize. The island is watching you. It has come to regard you as something akin to a slavegirl or concubine and, in its covetousness, will permit no rescuer to come to your aid. You are trapped. In a bid to make yourself unattractive to the island, you rub mud and fecalmatter upon your lovely face.

You starve yourself down to a mere shadow and mutilate your breasts with a flint. All to no avail. How can you step out of the island's gaze when every leaf and every grain of sand is a vessel of its lust? And what if you should die here? Will the island not take possession of you in a more permanent and, indeed, sexual fashion when your corpse disintegrates and bonds with the very soil?

6e. Thwarted in all your efforts to emancipate yourself, you formulate a more radical plan. You decide to swim out into the ocean, bringing with you only your flotation device and your memoirs. You pick the leeward side of the island, where the breakers are smallest, as the best launch-site for this venture. You know that you will almost certainly die in the effort, for you have seen no neighbouring islands in the distance and no passing ships, but as long as you swim far enough into the currents you will have escaped your captor. And escape, at this point, is your only desire. Do you truly believe freedom to be more important than survival or are you, in at least some measure, trying to spite the island? And if the latter, are there not other ways to achieve the same end? Name three great artistic achievements that have been made by persons in bondage and compare their respective milieus to your own.

6f. The night before your escape-attempt, you have a vivid dream of spacewalk. In the dream, you are a crew member aboard an Earth-orbiting shuttlecraft and you have been ordered to make repairs to the craft's exterior. As you step from the airlock into the void of space, you feel an elation unlike anything you have known before. You laugh like a child. Gazing down at the sleeping Earth, you recite the names of passing landforms and bodies of water. You see a meteorite transform into a needle of flame as it falls headlong through the atmosphere. Soon, however, you remember that this is only a dream and that when morning comes you will die. You go to the damaged portion of the spacecraft and begin to perform the requisite repairs. You work with slow and excessive diligence, hoping to make the dream last as long as possible. What is a pulsar? At what stellar distance does the mean radius of the Earth's orbit subtend an angle of seven seconds arc? Under what conditions do objects at points $L_4$ and $L_5$ of a Lagrange configuration remain stationary in relation to the primary gravitational bodies?

7. You are a timid and impoverished dweller of the forest. You live with your identical twin sister in a ramshackle cabin, foraging and trapping small game for sustenance. Both you and your sister are hideously deformed. It is for this reason that you live as outcasts. Your native town is only an hour's walk from the edge of the forest, but you have little contact with the townsfolk. They regard you

with deep-seated contempt, as if your deformities were the source of their every misfortune. The only reason they do not march upon your home and burn it to the ground is that violence against you has been forbidden by the town elders, who know all too well the value of a local scapegoat. This, then, is the ugly symbiosis that you have achieved with the townsfolk: you and your sister act as a repository for their ills and they, in turn, permit you to live.

7a. Your sister's name is Bev Rags. In truth, she was born Louise, but she has not answered to that name since childhood. You can remember clearly the day that you and she renounced your given names and, by extension, the world that bestowed them. A party of armed villagers had come to your childhood home, word of your hidden presence having spread throughout the district. Faced with the wrath of her neighbours, your mother pretended that you and your sister were not her own but, rather, two lost urchins whom she had sheltered out of pity. And she thrashed you like dogs until the townsfolk were satisfied that you were no flesh of hers. The mob then dragged you to the edge of town and banished you to the forest. What is your outcast name and what was your inspiration for naming yourself thus? What, ideally, would be your preferred means of destroying the documents that bore your given name: burial, shredding, or incineration? Explain your preference.

7b. It was during those initial years of exile that you and your sister invented Clarion. Clarion is the city of the deformed. Its streets and plazas are thronged with nature's most outlandish variations on the human figure and no two citizens are shaped alike. The philosophers of Clarion view the conventional human anatomy as a mere armature, a coat hanger from which is hung, in cases of the monstrous, a more singular and noble form. Were your parents or their fellow townsfolk to walk the city streets, they would be paragons of the most grotesque ugliness. Doubly so because their ugliness is the ugliness of the mundane. For what trades and special crafts are the people of Clarion renowned? On what is their economy based? How sophisticated is the city's underworld and where do conventional notions of beauty figure into its activities?

7c. These latter years of your spinsterhood have brought a series of unwelcome changes. The townsfolk have expanded their zone of hunting and foraging into territory that has traditionally been yours. And the weather has been droughtish all year. The end result is that you and your sister do not have enough food to last through the winter. In the course of a long and heated discussion, the two of you agree that you have no choice but to make contact with the townsfolk and initiate some kind of commerce. It is upon the nature of that commerce that you fundamentally disagree. Your sister believes that you should steal from the townsfolk using a sophisticated confidence scheme. You, on the other hand, propose to sell handcrafted toys to the town children. Whose idea is the surer road to profit? Do you object to your sister's plan on fiscal grounds alone and, if not, what is the true source of your misgivings?

7d. Toymaking is a skill that does not come easily to you, and the quality of your initial efforts is heartrendingly bad. The turning point comes when you decide to depict the inhabitants of Clarion. Even then, your carvings are squat and crude, but clumsiness of hand befits the hunchbacks and cretins that are your subject matter. More importantly, the toys succeed in capturing the imagination of the town's children. You establish with them a scheme of exchanging toys for food. From week to week, you leave a handful of carvings, accompanied by an empty foodbasket, upon the nearest of the town boundary stones. Initially, the children are reluctant to enter into the proposed transaction, but soon, as the popularity of your toys gains traction among them, they become more bold. And within weeks many of them are playing truant in order to keep watch over the boundary stone. Why are the children attracted to such strange and grotesque playthings? Have they no other outlet for their morbid leanings? How does your exploitation of their morbidity affect your self-regard and do you fear that they will think badly of you later in life?

7e. Meanwhile, your sister has begun an enterprise of her own. She has learned that there are hierarchies at work even within the world of the not-deformed and that men of the lowest orders will gladly pay for a woman's favours, be she ugly or be she ill. She has even learned of deviants who prefer her twisted flesh to that of the town's most voluptuous maidens. She sells herself to these men, meeting them in a grove halfway between your hut and the town proper. A woman of the world now, she laughs at you and your little carvings. She boasts of her relative wealth and of her aptitude for picking the pockets of her clientele. Is your sister's tendency toward thievery a matter of mere financial gain, or does robbing her clients procure for her some other, less tangible, dividend? Describe the psychological mechanism by which a man might come to lust after deformed flesh alone.

7f. Inevitably, your sister's recklessness provokes the ire of the townsfolk. She steals from one of her customers a sum of money great enough that he would rather confess to his dalliance with a prostitute than see her escape justice. Thus ends the delicate balance. A collective rage consumes the townsfolk and they march upon your home with torches and machetes. When they arrive, however, they find you there alone, for your sister has fled and left you to bear the consequences of her actions. You fall to your knees and beg for mercy. You offer to pay back all the money that your sister has stolen, but the townsfolk have come for blood, not gold, and blood alone will appease them. Will your sister hear from her hiding place in the woods your shrill and pitiful screams? Will her flesh, through the miracle of twinship, transform into a map of your torments? Does she possess adequate force of character to take vengeance upon the townsfolk or will she drift like a phantom into the deep, uncharted woods?

7g. In the city of Clarion, a child is born. It is a long labour, and no sooner has the infant begun to wail than a nursemaid wraps him in a towel and ferries him away into the night. Her destination is the outer suburbs, a land of scrap yards and heavy industry. In the hiddenmost reaches of a decommissioned chemical plant, she opens a nondescript steel door and takes the infant down into a cellar where a grey and sombre dormitory has been arrayed on the concrete floor. The children gathered there observe this new arrival with studied indifference. These children are symmetrical of feature, their bodies bereft of horns and supernumary limbs. In any other world they would be exemplars of pediatric health and beauty. Why are they hidden here, as if their existence were a dark and shameful thing? Are you an adherent of segregation and, if not, why do you permit it to occur? Has death not made you the goddess of Clarion? Are the tectonics of this world not yours to manipulate as you please, its hubris yours to punish at will?

8.  I have decided to commit suicide. My goal is to end my life in a manner so singular that it requires no explanatory note, the manner of death proclaiming in action all that I could hope to say in words. Having led a long and lucrative career in the field of high finance, I have sufficient funds to enlist whatever assistance I might require. My first step, then, is to form a suicide committee. Over the course of eight months, the suicide committee solicits and evaluates some twenty bids for the contract to end my life. And from the final shortlist of three, a winner is chosen. The winning firm then begins development of the various installations required in order to bring its plan to fruition. Late one evening, some three years later, I receive word that everything is ready. The next morning I rise from bed, eat a hearty breakfast and make my way to the place of execution. The drive takes me through the deep cool of the pinewoods north of the city. During the final stretch of the journey, a deer steps out into the road. I swerve to avoid it and, in so doing, lose control of my car.

8a. I wake up in hospital. A doctor comes to my bedside and asks me a battery of questions. Throughout this interrogation, my mind is hazy, my powers of recollection poor. The doctor tells me that my name is Balthazar. Prompted thus, I am flooded with a chain of recollections. Balthazar is indeed my name and I am ten years old. I have no siblings and my mother is dead. The doctor gives me a sip of water and asks how I came to have so many bruises. I tell him that

I got my bruises accidentally, while playing.
In answering thus, how many direct lies have
I just told? How many indirect? How, in fact,
did I get my bruises and by what inspiration did
my parents name me Balthazar?

8b. Later in the day, my father comes to bring me
home from the hospital. He is dishevelled and
taciturn and I can tell that he is put out by the
task of collecting me. No sooner have we arrived
home than he begins a new drinking binge.
I go up to my bedroom and read until dark, at
which point I turn off the light and seat myself
at the window. Downstairs, my father begins to
mutter aloud. As his drunkenness intensifies,
his rantings become more vociferous and
lose like pocketchange their initial coherence.
Sometime after midnight, he falls asleep in his
chair. What is the lure of oblivion? Do children
not require it with the intensity of adults, or
is our lesser incidence of alcoholism a simple
consequence of our restricted access to spirits?
And when children require oblivion, to whom
or what can they turn?

8c. I gaze out into the night. Our house sits alone
on the shore of a small, almond-shaped lake.
It is deepest winter and the water is frozen
solid, the trees about all glittering with snow.
An abandoned carousel sits atop the ice at the
centre of the lake. It appeared there earlier this
winter, its origins a mystery. By now its impaled
and weatherworn horses have become a fixture

of my every waking thought, an obsession. I sit rapt at the window, concocting dark histories of carnivals and conmen, until the hour grows late and my eyes begin to shut of their own accord. I lie down in bed and fall asleep. Am I the kind of child who sleeps loglike until morning, or do I wake at intervals throughout the night? Do nightmares take hold of me at every turn and, if so, what is their content?

8d. The next morning, I make breakfast for my father and then go outside to chop wood. I chop enough for three bales of kindling and bring the wood into the house. As I deposit the third bale beside the fireplace, my father rises from his chair and strikes me in the face. I fall to the floor. He kicks me repeatedly, telling me that I have cut too much kindling and that I am wasting his money. I promise to pay for the wastage, but this only enhances his rage. He takes an ember from the fire and puts it down the front of my trousers. I make horrible, doglike screams, the utterance of which immediately fills me with shame. What is the key to remaining silent while undergoing a course of ordeal? Is this knowledge given to commandoes and secret agents alone? Should it not also be made available to children like myself, at least until such time as our safety can be vouchsafed?

8e. I spend the rest of the day in my room, waiting for night. Darkness falls and, once I am certain that my father is asleep, I rise and dress for the cold. I put my good watch on my left wrist and my old, broken watch on my right. I go downstairs, collect my boots and leave the house. It is a cold, windy night and the snow crumbles ashlike under my feet. I walk out to the beach and shuffle across the frozen lake to the carousel. I walk clockwise around the platform, touching all the horses and giving each one a secret name. In the end, I choose a chestnut horse that looks as if it were made especially for a boy my size. I seat myself on the horse and use my bootlaces to tie my feet into the stirrups. I wrap my arms around the horse's neck and fasten my two watch-straps together so that my wrists are held tight, as if handcuffed. The carousel begins to spin. Over a course of mere minutes, it accelerates to a dizzying speed, as if to fling away all timid and unsure riders. The lights burn brightly and the organ plays a wild and heedless tune. The carousel, in having sprung to life, has shown me unusual favour and for this I am grateful. At the same time, however, I feel a deep and desolate sadness. Why is sadness always co-present in my most intense experiences of joy? Does it give context and permanence to otherwise fleeting pleasures, or have I simply become estranged from the experience of pure delight? And, if the latter, how can I be repaired?

8f. The ice begins to break. Initially, the carousel holds fast and for a time I fear that it is not heavy enough to pierce through. But in the end it falls.

It topples sidelong into the water, like something undermined, and sinks quickly beneath the waves. The cold squeezes me breathless in its grim and silver fist. A week from now, my schoolteacher will report me missing. A party of rangers will comb the woods and divers will gather on the shoreline. After days of fruitless searching, they will find me at the lakebottom lashed hand and foot to my faithful steed. And the image of me will haunt them for the rest of their days. With great clarity and purity of intent I have taken my own life. Is this a terrible thing for me to have done? Prescribe me an alternative. Delineate for me a future in which I shall regain the eloquence I possess tonight as a child who chooses self-destruction.

9. Walking home from a night of shopping, you are kidnapped by members of a religious cult. The cultists drug you to sleep and ferry you away to their compound in the mountains. Inside the compound, you awaken in a clean and sparsely-furnished cell. At first light an old woman comes to your bedside bearing food and fresh water. Her name is Marielle. Appointed to act as your guide, she attempts to provide you with a brief explanation of both the cult's ideology and the rationale for your abduction. The cult is called the Voice of the Worm and its members worship the process of decay. The first pillar of their beliefs is that beauty and reason are loathsome aberrations from the formless chaos that is the universe's right and fundamental state. Hence the call-and-response that begins their Mass:

| MINISTER: | "My light is the scar tissue and the toothless maw." |
| CONGREGATION: | "And not the face of youth." |
| MINISTER: | "When genius totters into neverending dotage." |
| CONGREGATION: | "Then shall I rejoice." |

The cultists have abducted you because their scouts have designated you a model of contemporary wit and beauty. And only someone who possesses these traits in their purest form can properly experience the purest form of their loss. Today you will be required to undergo an ordeal in the cult's most holy temple. If you pass the ordeal, you will be crowned high priestess over the entire cult, your every order to be obeyed without question. If you fail the ordeal or refuse to comply with its administration, you will be executed.

9a. Members of the cult then lead you away to the temple. In a backroom adjoining the main chapel, they seat you at a desk, the surface of which is clear but for a pen, a notebook and a cup of tea. The cultists tell you that your first task is to write a letter to your loved ones, renouncing your kinship with them in the strongest possible terms. You will be graded on cruelty, abandon and originality of expression. The tea, they explain, is a special psychoactive brew called Nightsbreath. It is crafted by a secret inner guild for the purpose of inducing dysphoria during the cult's high rituals of the solstice and eclipse. Drinking it will help you to compose your letter with a suitable level of conviction. Why is the tea called Nightsbreath and how do its effects compare with other forms of intoxication that you have known? Does it, in fact, help you to write your letter? Provide here a seventy-five- to one-hundred-word sample of your screed, clearly indicating in the margins which passages are written with sincerity, which are written with artifice and which are written with some greater or lesser admixture of the two.

9b. Next, they paint your face with a strange and foulsmelling lotion that numbs your flesh like lidocaine. They take you to a small, unfurnished room where a red steel toolbox sits in the middle of the floor. The cultists explain to you that the toolbox contains the pieces of a jigsaw puzzle. Your task is to solve the puzzle as quickly as possible, even though there is no key image to guide you. Emptying the puzzle pieces onto the floor, you find them to be faintly luminous, like things irradiated. You begin the process of assembly. As the minutes pass, however, the puzzle begins to discharge an ever fiercer and more menacing grade of brightness. And soon you must work with eyes clenched shut for fear of being blinded. In this advanced stage of incandescence, the puzzle pieces become hot to the touch and your fingertips hiss whilst manipulating them. Your final seconds in this phase of the ordeal are spent bathed in a coronal, magnesium-white light: the puzzle shines up at you, seething and unfinished, and your face burns openly as if plunged into a blastfurnace. What image does the jigsaw puzzle form? What effect would successful completion of the puzzle have had upon its properties of luminosity and heat? Explain briefly the mechanics of magical pictures and the apparatus by which they induce physiological change.

9c. You awaken sprawled upon a bed of straw, a fever raging firelike through your body. Marielle sits at your bedside, sponging water onto your broken lips. You reach up to touch your face and find that the burns on your cheeks and forehead have swollen into knotlike configurations of edema. The swellings are insensate and frighteningly turgid, like wayward outcroppings of bone. You know intuitively the moment you touch them that your face will remain forever deformed. Marielle takes note of your distress and tells you not to worry. "As the Nightsbreath takes proper hold of your mind," she says, "your wit will shrivel to nothing at all. You will lose all memory of your pretty face and your pretty life and the pretty friends who were nowhere near to help you at the moment when you most needed them." Has your memory indeed begun to fail? Close your eyes and try to recall your surroundings in perfect detail. What colour are Marielle's eyes? Describe her attire. How many framed paintings adorn the walls of this room and what does each depict?

9d. The cultists take you down into the temple basement. The floor is bare dirt and they lead you across it to a grave that they have dug in the far corner of the room. At the bottom of the grave lies the corpse of a young woman. She is naked, her body contorted into a painful-looking and vaguely pugilistic posture like that of someone poisoned. Her features are masked by a life-scale photograph of your face as it appeared at the apotheosis of its lost beauty. The cultists inform you that this is their former high priestess. Your final task is to bury her. They hand you a shovel and you commence to inter the masked and naked stranger under the dirt piled at graveside for this purpose. Your body is tired from the day's ordeal, but fear of the cultists lends you new and redoubled vigour. You sweat like a packmule and strain the muscles of your arms and back as you struggle to move the dirt to its target. During the final minutes of your task, the cultists file from the room, as if having sensed that you will soon breach forth into territories where they cannot follow. As if your final ascent into contact with the godhead were a thing not fit for them to see. For how long did the woman in the pit hold the office of high priestess? Conjecture what events might have precipitated her downfall. What is most likely to end your own reign: insurrection, abdication or expiry of allotted term? Explain your choice.

9e. When at last the grave is full, you tamp down
the dirt and climb the stairs to the ground floor.
Outside, bundled neatly on the temple steps,
are your shopping bags and the purse that you
were carrying when abducted. You pick up these
items and hold them tightly to your chest as you
wander through the dusk. The compound has
the air of a place long deserted. The windows
are dark and shuttered from without and the
cellars have been emptied of all provisions.
Even the sentries have abandoned their posts,
their assault rifles lying in the dust or propped
like sticks against the ramparts. You return to
your cell. You try to formulate a plan of action,
but the action of the Nightsbreath has crippled
your intellect. You fear the coming darkness like
a common diapered half-wit. You bellow with
hunger, the logistics of scavenging for food
and firewood too complex for your poisoned
mind. Terrified by the sight of your ruined face,
you drive your fist through the mirror above
the sink. And when you see in the resulting
pool of fragments a hundred fresh multiples
of the same hideous image, you take a long
and talon-shaped shard of glass and use it to
gouge out your eyes. Picture for a moment the
twin goddesses of the cult: they sit enthroned
upon a mountain of garbage, one to rule over
the land of the living, the other over the land
of the dead. What would they make of this last,
spontaneous mutilation? Is it a fitting act of
faith or a sacrilege or both? Consider a question
from the goddesses' own mouths: "Is despair

the only appropriate response to the day's ordeal, or is there not also grounds to celebrate, your newfound ugliness and smallness of mind making you kin to a greater part of humankind than beauty and intelligence ever could have done?"

9f. Your screams draw the attention of a passing woodsman. He follows your voice down the mountainside and finds you howling like an animal on the floor of your cell. Though he suspects you instantly for a madwoman and fears that you will turn upon him with violence, he approaches you without hesitation in order to stanch the bleeding of your eyesockets. Using the radio in the room next door, he calls for help. And whilst the two of you await medivac, he sits beside you on the bloody and glass-strewn floor, holding you close and humming a tune he half recalls from the fog of his distant childhood. When at last you are calm and silent, he ventures to ask you why you have enucleated yourself. You tell him about the cultists and their mutilation of your face. You tell him that by virtue of having passed their ordeal you have become their high priestess, the living embodiment of all they hold divine. As the sound of the rescue helicopter draws near, you vouch to the woodsman that you will always remember him for the kindness he has shown you on this night. Wherever he might wander in the years to come, you will shower him with bounty and good fortune. How does a priestess of your type and temperament reward her most worthy devotees? Why, as the medics take you away, does the woodsman look so forlorn? Why can he not see your deformities, your face appearing to him in all its lost and exquisite beauty save the puncture wounds that you yourself have inflicted upon each eye?

9g. Standing like a shockvictim in the wreckage of your cell, the woodsman notices your purse. The objects contained therein inspire him to take a journey. The next morning, he drives to your home using your own identification to find the address and your own set of keys to gain entry. The house's interior is musty and still, like that of a place too long unaired. The woodsman collects your mail from the floor and places it on the kitchen counter. He waters your plants. He walks slowly through the house, detective-style, looking for some sign or clue that will reveal to him the roots of your insanity. The photographs that adorn the walls and mantelpiece are of particular interest to him and he spends long minutes standing before each, gazing like a widower into your longlost eyes. As darkness falls, he goes up to your bedroom and lies down on the bed fully clothed. Drifting like a drug addict on the fragrance of your skin and hair, he has a terrible thought: he will build in this world a correlate to every figment of your diseased imagination. If there is no cult called the Voice of the Worm, then he will create one. If there is no woman interred in the temple basement, then he will put one there himself and in so doing set to rights your slippage from the world. With that thought, the woodsman falls asleep. He dreams that he has come to visit you in the padded asylum cell where you will live out the rest of your days. You command him to remove your straitjacket and he complies, though he knows that he should not. The straitjacket is your skin now, your exoskeleton, and without it you will die. As he unfastens the first buckle, you begin to bleed. And with every strap he loosens thereafter, bundles of muscle and fat and flesh drop raglike from under the canvas. Will the woodsman awaken from this dream in ecstasy or terror and how will he interpret its course? What setbacks drove him to live on the mountain, apart from his fellow man? When will he realize that he has fallen in love with you, that your entry into his life has made a farce of his ostensible contentment, his ostensible hunger for solitude and peace of mind?

10. You are ninety-four years old. You have been hospitalized. Like a sere and broken bird, you lie alone in a far corner of the palliative ward, your organs tottering on the verge of failure. Your mind has slipped into perpetual twilight, a frightened incomprehension like that of a caged or injured beast. Daytime is a gauntlet of rough hygiene and pain, the petty humiliation of caregivers who speak of you as if you were already dead. But the nights are far worse. As daylight fades, the stains of old effluvia bloom darkly on the crumbling walls and floor. Cribdeath and gangrene stride wraithlike

through the wards. The darkness is a tactile thing. It weighs upon you like waterpressure, it pools in your lungs like fumes from a distant star.

10a. In these last nights before your death, you become a sleepwalker. Like a common insomniac, you steal from your bed in the lifeless hours of early morning and go wandering through the halls. Your carriage is erect and your stride is true, your body completely and utterly beguiled by its dream of wellness. And you are lucid throughout. Is this your first experience of somnambulism? Have you in the course of your life been prone to fits or spells or seizures of any stripe? What is it like to relinquish authorship of your steps and do you long all the while for the safety of your bed?

10b. On the first night, you go to the psychiatric ward. The nurses' station is unattended. You help yourself to a passkey and enter the locked and half-lit sector where patients are kept on suicide watch. In one of the rooms, a woman with a bandaged throat gapes witlessly at the ceiling. Her chart informs you that she is a brothel-keeper. Her age is listed as forty-two years, but she looks much older. You enter the room and, in a clear and steady voice, announce to the woman the current address of the son she gave up for adoption some two and a half decades ago. "He lives alone," you tell her:

He has a melancholy turn of mind (something I need not describe to you) and has, in truth, fared poorly in this life. He works in a manufacturing plant for a pitiful wage. His friends are dullards and he has no talent for meeting women. I will not waste time with talk of reconciliation, with exhortations that you go to him and reclaim the maternal role. But consider a left-handed reunion. Consider subterfuge. Three blocks west of the building where he lives is the regional headquarters of an international work-study program. Obtain some samples of the program's literature and, in the guise of a volunteer engaged in door-to-door canvassing, go to your son's apartment. Convince him to abandon his drudgery and start a new life overseas. He is ripe for the suggestion, but he will not dislodge himself without your encouragement. And without an upheaval of this or greater magnitude, he will, I fear, die a wastrel's death.

How is it that you know so much about the young man in question? Or do the words spring from your mouth unbidden? Describe the sensation of uttering them. For whom or what are you acting as cypher?

10c. On the second night, you go to the emergency department. In one of the supply closets, a sixty-two-year-old porter stands on a stepladder, stocking the shelves with gloves and gowns. You approach the porter and tell him to cease work immediately. "I must speak with you on a matter of the utmost gravity," you tell him:

In a month's time, you will be involved in a car accident which, though minor by pure forensic standards, will have disastrous consequences for your long-term health. Blunt force injuries to your legs and back will leave you saddled with intense chronic pain. You will no longer be able to engage in any form of gainful employment. As such, and despite your best efforts to coddle your meagre disability pension, the savings that you have amassed over the course of your working life will begin to dwindle rather than accrue. And within the span of a few short years, you will be penniless. If indeed you still aim to return to your homeland and to the town where you were born, you must go now. You believe yourself not to have saved sufficient funds to buy a house, but in this you are mistaken. The woman who taught you grades one through four still lives in the cottage at the edge of town. She wishes to move away in order to be with her children. She remembers you. She does not lack for money and would rather sell her home to a familiar for less than market value than see it fall into the hands of a stranger.

Is it common for schoolteachers to remember a student from so many years ago? What might the porter have done, as a boy, in order to distinguish himself? What additional force will your words have if he recalls having set foot in that very house, delivering perhaps a card on his teacher's birthday or taking subscriptions for the newspaper?

10d. Your third night's wanderings take you down to the burn unit. As you step through the doors, you feel a change in the air. This is a place bereaved of hope, a zone of limitless, unremitting pain. You see a girl in a plastic tent. A single glance suffices to tell you that she is on the verge of death. Her body is impossibly small, the flesh ragged and raw like something worked over by dogs. Even her eyes are burnt. You pull a chair up to the girl's bedside and speak to her in a low, conspiratorial tone:

It is a familiar story: the act of violence that brought you here was an aberration, a random tragedy that could just as easily have befallen any other girl. But, deep down, you do not believe this to be true. Deep down, you know that you have always been different from those around you and that your destiny, once revealed, would be a special one. Tonight I am authorized to confirm that the life you have led up until now has been nothing but a flimsy, if well-intentioned, charade. Outside these hospital walls, the world is burning. In the events about to unfold, your kind alone shall be fit to occupy the roles at centre stage because you alone know first hand the terrors of fire and shrapnel. At this very moment, the members of your true family are travelling here to join you. They had always hoped that you could learn of your destiny at leisure and in a more commodious setting, but time has run short. The battle is underway and your return to the fold has become a matter of great urgency. Come with me.

What is the principal difference between the words you have spoken to the girl and those that you spoke to the mental patient and the porter? Does the girl's youth augment or diminish her ability to take the leap of faith requested? Does her condition?

10e. You tear open the girl's sterile tent and prepare an injection. Morphine for her pain, dexedrine for langour. You administer the injection and help her to get out of bed. The two of you walk hand in hand to the main entrance of the hospital, the girl leaving bloody footprints in her wake. As you step outside, you see that the entire surrounding cityscape has been obliterated. Everything outside the hospital grounds has been reduced to ruins by a great, apocalyptic fire. "Listen carefully," you say to the girl:

Over this first mound of rubble is a broad tract of level ground. A column of smoke stands rising in the distance. That is the epicentre of the bombing. Walk toward it and within a period of two to three hours you will come to a zone as flat as a meadow where even the chimneystacks have been knocked to the ground. Unlike the screaming injured of these outer regions, the ones you encounter there will be silent and immobile, blackened to the flesh as if in mourning for themselves. Leave them to their sleep. Beware of sinkholes and the small avalanches of ash and brick by which this city shall continue in the weeks ahead to collapse in upon itself. When you reach the crater at the centre of the destruction, write your name on a piece of fireblackened wood—blood is the only acceptable ink—and place it in the mouth of a deadman. That is the signal. Your family will come for you then. They will answer all of your questions.

You let go of the girl's hand and push her forward. Twice, as she makes her way to the edge of the grounds, she turns to look back at you. Both times you wave her sternly away. She climbs up the mound of blackened rubble and disappears over the top. You stand guard for several minutes and, once you are certain that she will not return, you go back into the hospital. What, indeed, will become of the girl?

Who or what awaits her in the crater at ground zero? And what of the burnt-out world that your tale has unleashed: will it hold? Is its autonomy sufficient for it to function on its own, or will it collapse at the moment of your death into a heap of pretty lies?

10f. You return to the palliative ward and lie down in bed. The past three nights of wandering have left you in a dangerously weakened state. Exhausted, you close your eyes. In the slow and gentle drifting toward death, you imagine that you are not a widow dying of simple old age but rather a young woman in the grip of a baleful, all-consuming passion. A love with no outlet runs rampant through your body, killing you slowly like some rare and ultralethal toxin. It is a happy thought. You speak aloud:

> I slept late again this morning and left the bed in disarray. I rearranged the books on my shelves for the third time this week. As the whistle blew for the evening shift, I became restless and went walking along the concourse. The faces of your colleagues were antic things, pockmarked little cabinets of numbness and rage. In the corridor outside the nineteenth chamber I saw a group of examiners preparing a new test subject for the ordeal within. She looked to be little more than a child. The examiners recognized me and paused in their work, the leader raising his eyebrows

interrogatively as I approached. Yes, I said, of course I will take her place. An hour later, I stepped out of the chamber, bright with conquered pain. The examiners looked at me with pitying eyes, as if I were somehow deficient. As if they had never before seen a woman admiring her fresh new scars. Back in my room, your letters gaze back at me from where I have tacked them to the wall. I have annotated every passage, provided chronologies and explanatory footnotes. The evidence is incontrovertible: not only are we meant to be together but, in your heart of hearts, you know this to be true. Come home soon. I have cut away like tumourcells all my weakness and my fear. I am an amputee comprised solely of violence and beauty and the hunger to be by your side.

Why do we devote more passion to the loves that destroy us than we do to the loves that heal us and make us complete? Is it inevitable that we should conduct ourselves thus? Imagine that your death brings no respite from desire, that it pitches you into wilder, more potent states of longing. Though they bury you alone beneath the cold and final earth, you shall burn for the touch of your every unsung love. Discuss.

JASON HRIVNAK lives and works in Toronto.
*The Plight House* is his first novel.